THE GOLD CURSE

Other Books by the Author

The Gold Solution
The Gold Deadline
The Gold Frame

THE GOLD CURSE

A WHODUNIT

Herbert Resnicow

A
JOAN
KAHN
BOOK

St. Martin's Press
New York

Design by Amy Bernstein

Library of Congress Cataloging-in-Publication Data

Resnicow, Herbert.
    The gold curse.
    "A Joan Kahn Book"
    I. Title.
PS3568.E69G55   1986   813'.54   86-3660
ISBN 0-312-33678-0

Copyeditor: Eva Galan Salmieri

First Edition

10 9 8 7 6 5 4 3 2 1

To Joan Kahn
The Dean of Deans
Who Spun Dross into Gold.

THE GOLD
CURSE

1

"I want a gun," I told the salesman, "that I can carry in my bra." He was already forming the fatal word when I saw he was wearing a wedding band, so I decided to save his life. "If the word *howitzer* crosses your lips," I said politely, "there will be a head-shaped dent in that expensive-looking shotgun on the rack."

"I was about to say, madame"—he recovered neatly—"how would you like a derringer?"

"Positively not," I said, remembering what a derringer had done to me in the Talbott case. "I'm not a sharpshooter, and I may need more than two shots."

He smiled confidently. "Then what you want is a Beretta Model 20 Double Action Semiautomatic Pistol. No manual hammer cocking is required and it has an inertia-type firing pin. A perfect belly gun."

Every time a woman sets foot in a so-called masculine preserve, especially if it's not by choice, the filthy little beasts start with the technical jargon. It's supposed to put you in your place, wherever that is. Hah! That will be the day when Norma Gold, ex-super-research-librarian, can be put down by a skinny child a head shorter and fifty pounds lighter, with an IQ of, maybe, triple his age, tops. Especially since I had stopped in at the library last week and researched the whole *schmeer*.

"I do not intend"—I gave him my dowager duchess look— "to waste my hard-earned money on overpriced, snob-appeal, gold-plated, designer-initialed, fancy imported junk. I need a practical gun for my work." That would make him take notice. "Let me see a Browning 25 Automatic. The Lightweight Model."

"May I ask what your work is, madame, and what purpose the weapon is to serve?"

"I'm a licensed private investigator, young man, and when some creep is trying to kill me or my partner, or even my husband, I want to kill that creep first."

"How far away will your assailant be, do you think?"

"Anywhere from right next to me to across a big room."

"May I suggest a larger caliber weapon, then? A nine-millimeter?"

"I used a .32 on the range when I was practicing to get my carry license. A .32 is too big and heavy to carry easily, and it kicks too hard. I'm still a woman, you know," I said, turning a little so he could get the full force of my riveting profile, "and I want a woman's gun."

He lifted his eyes back up to mine. "They call these little .25-caliber automatics belly guns, madame, because many people stick them into the front of their belt. But some people say they're called belly guns because the only way you can be sure of hitting someone is to stick the gun right into his belly before you pull the trigger."

"Are you telling me that a belly gun is useless if my target is twenty feet away?"

"These little automatics are not accurate over ten feet and usually cause very little damage over twenty feet."

"One of them," I pointed out, "did a lot of damage to the president and his press secretary from over twenty feet away."

"That was pure accident, madame. It takes an expert to use one of these effectively."

I didn't want to hear any more. It had really cost me just to decide to get a gun; completely against all my principles. On the practice range I had to keep telling myself, "It's only a target, a piece of cardboard." Now, actually standing in a gun shop, surrounded by guns, guns which would be used to kill people . . . In spite of what I had said to Pearl and Alexander, I didn't really *want* a gun. What I wanted was to make sure that no one hurt Alexander. Or Pearl. I had to get out of that store fast, before I lost control. "Wrap up a Browning Lightweight," I told the clerk. "I want to take it with me. Here are the papers."

He didn't move. "Madame," he said, "I understand what you want, but I think the Beretta will be better for you. May I explain why?"

Everything was working against me; no way to just get my gun and go. He'd have to have his say. I nodded wearily. "The Beretta," he said, "is only three ounces heavier than the Browning and an inch longer. It's a modern gun, very well made. Its magazine carries eight rounds while the Browning only carries six."

"The extra weight and length may not seem like much to you," I said, "but I don't have much spare space in my bra."

"May I ask, madame, why you want to carry a gun in such an unusual place?"

"I won't always be wearing clothes that will hide a shoulder holster or a belt holster. Or an ankle holster either. And I don't want to walk the way I'd have to wearing a thigh holster."

"Most women carry their guns in their bags."

"You can forget the gun when you change bags. Or the bag can be left somewhere. Or stolen. A bra you always wear; or, at least, I do. Besides, if I'm searched, no one would find it there. Or dare to look."

"You might have difficulty getting it out fast, madame."

"I won't be wearing high-cut blouses in the future. And I do have bras with lots of separation."

He looked stubborn. "I suggest, madame, that you first buy a toy gun and try wearing it in your bra for a day. Then, in the privacy of your home, try getting the gun out fast. See how long it takes you, and then visualize what your attacker could do to you or your partner in that time. Or your husband."

I knew he was right. I had enough trouble carrying *myself* in my bra; an extra lump would be a real pain. "All right," I said, "you win. Give me the Beretta; I'll carry it in my bag." I handed him the permit.

"But Mrs. Gold," he said, "this is made out for the Browning."

"I had it made out in advance purposely, so I could go home with a gun today." I had planned it as a surprise for Alexander, and had invited Pearl and Burton over for supper to witness the unveiling. "So give me the Browning; it's what I really wanted in the first place."

"We don't carry that model, Mrs. Gold. They stopped making it a long time ago."

"Then give me the Beretta; I'll get the permit changed on Monday."

"I'm not allowed to do that, Mrs. Gold. It's illegal."

"You mean I can't get a gun right now?"

"Only what's on your permit."

"But it's an antique, you said."

"Hardly that; a collector's model, but rather costly. You could get two Berettas for the price of one of those."

I was beginning to get the picture. "You wouldn't be a collector, by any chance, would you?"

4

"All people in this business are collectors, to a certain extent."

"And would you, by any chance, have in your collection a Browning 25 Automatic Lightweight?"

"Not just in my collection, madame. I carry it in my belt holster, in back. Because of its size, you know. It doesn't spoil the drape of my jacket. And I'm an expert shot with it, unlike most people. Would you like to see it?" He reached behind himself smoothly and the tiny silver gun was on the counter. He kept it out of my reach, with his hand hovering over it. "It's loaded," he explained. "Everyone who works in a gun shop must be licensed. Sometimes people wander in, people who look perfectly normal . . ."

"Sell me your gun. I'll pay anything."

He looked shocked and immediately put the gun back behind him. "My life may depend on this gun."

"You can get a Beretta easy; you work here."

"I'd have to get my permit changed. Come back late Tuesday; I'll sell it to you then."

I broke down. "I can't wait three days. Please? Please? My husband had a terrible heart attack last year and almost died. Then a murderer shot me. Another one tried to strangle my husband. Then Pearl was almost killed. My partner." I couldn't help crying; after all I had gone through and expecting to just walk in and buy the gun and . . . "I can't wait till Tuesday. If someone attacks my husband tonight and I don't have a gun . . . Please, *now*. I'll do anything you want, pay anything . . . anything."

He looked at me for a while, then took out the gun, unloaded it, and put it on the counter. "I didn't realize," he said. "I'm sorry you're so upset. The price is what I said before, no more. That's what it's worth; you can check. I'll carry a Beretta illegally until Tuesday. Let's just hope I don't have to use it." He took the holster off his belt and put the little gun into it.

"Thank you," I said, "thank you. I really . . . I'm sorry I was so . . . before. It's just that, with all my worries . . . and my husband . . . He gets excited, sometimes, and his heart . . . He thinks nothing can hurt him, no one. I have to take care of everyone."

"I understand, madame."

"You can keep the holster. I'm going to carry it in my bag."

"The holster is made for this gun, Mrs. Gold. I have no use for it. You never know when you'll need it."

"All right; thank you again. And I'll need some bullets too. Magnum."

He shook his head. "Not magnum. Not if you want to stop someone."

"When I was shot last year, it was two magnum slugs, .22 caliber, which is a lot smaller than .25. I was stopped, all right, almost permanently."

"That could happen, sometimes, but to really be sure you need a slow-moving slug, one which is deflected by any hard surface and wanders around inside the body causing all sorts of damage."

I was feeling sick again. He didn't have to be so damned explicit; we both knew what a gun was for. "All right"—I swallowed hard—"what should I use?"

"I'd suggest a Winchester 45 grain-expanding point. Aim at the torso and squeeze the trigger fast."

"Okay, I'll take a box. Also an extra magazine."

"There are no extra magazines; to get one you'd have to buy another gun. But don't bother. Under the conditions you described, if you can't stop him with six shots, you won't have time to change magazines. In fact, you'd be lucky to get one shot off. You still have to push the slide back first."

"No, I don't; I'm going to keep one bullet in the chamber all the time."

He really turned pale. "No! You musn't, madame. Nobody does that, nobody sane. You could easily shoot yourself."

"That's a thumb safety there, isn't it? And there's a magazine safety too; I read about it."

"The magazine safety works only when the magazine is out of the gun, and I know you're going to keep the magazine in the gun at all times. The thumb safety . . . One day you'll forget and . . . A very small trigger pull will fire the gun when it's cocked. Even dropping the gun may fire it. I won't sell you the gun if you . . . You must swear never to keep a bullet in the chamber."

I swore. Being married, I have been known to lie before. In a good cause. Such as to avoid an argument with Alexander. But if I ever have to shoot someone fast to save my husband's life, or even Pearl's, I'm not going to waste time pulling back slides. And that way I'd have seven shots instead of six. You never know.

2

The dinner was a great success, as usual. The trick, when you stuff squid, is to grind some fennel seed with hot pepper flakes. Heaven. Alexander had been stuck at 206 pounds for the past month—he had to be cheating but I hadn't caught him yet—so the desert was simply pears poached in red vermouth with a dab of real vanilla-seed custard in the hollow.

With Burton and Pearl, and especially Alexander, in a good stuffed mood, I announced, "I've been carrying a gun all evening. Anyone notice anything?"

"No," Burton said, "but a careful search—"

"Down, Rover," I said. "But Pearl can have the thrill."

"I can't reach it, Norma." My little blond partner was wearing low-heeled shoes for a relaxed evening. "But it has to be in your hair. You haven't worn it bouffant in years."

"Nope. Try again." I was wearing my blouse out, over my skirt; the belt holster had come in handy after all. It didn't feel bad, just a bit heavy. The hairdo was a red herring.

"It has to be a garter holster," Burton said. "You've been walking funny all evening. Like a student geisha with a book between her knees."

"What do you know about geishas?" Pearl asked. "You told me, when you travel, it's strictly business."

"When in Rome. . .," Burton said. "A lot of business gets done in a relaxed atmosphere, so a client needs his lawyer along. The things I do to keep my wife in sables." He sighed wearily.

"If it's that well hidden," Alexander pointed out, "it has to be very small, practically useless. And it'll take a long time to get out."

"Oh, yeah?" I said cleverly. "Watch this." I slipped my hand behind me and had the gun out in one second. There was no bullet in the chamber, naturally. This time.

"Be careful where you point that thing, Norma," Pearl said. "Is it loaded?"

"Of course," I said. "And I'm not pointing it at you."

"No, you're pointing it at your left bazoom. I know it's too big, Norma, but plastic surgery is much neater."

"You're jealous because you're flat-chested," I said, putting her in her place. At five feet nothing, stripped, 34D is adequate, but compared to me? Nothing.

"Would you really shoot a human being, Norma?" It had finally penetrated Pearl's little blond brain what the gun was for. "Last year we went around getting signatures to ban handguns. What happened to you?"

"I got shot," I said simply. "I still want to ban handguns, Pearl. For everybody, myself included. And I'm not going to shoot people just like that. But if someone tries to kill me, or you, or even Burton . . ." I purposely didn't mention Alexander. Now that he's gone back to gym again, God forbid I should even suggest that he needed protection.

"I still think"—my dear husband can't ever let me win—"that having a gun changes your attitude; makes you dependent on the weapon instead of yourself."

"Alexander's right," Pearl said. Just once I'd like to hear her say that Alexander's wrong. "When you need it most, a machine will fail you. Whereas your own body, if you keep in good shape"—she took a deep breath—"and have the right mental attitude, such as aikido develops in one, you will always be prepared to avoid harm."

"Has your Master taught you how to dodge bullets yet?" I asked, strictly in the spirit of free inquiry. "I hope it never happens, but if it does, you will thank me, someday. You will kiss the ground I walk on; you will—"

"If you're going to carry that thing on you all the time," Pearl said, "you can't wear a gown without a jacket."

"That's okay, Pearl. I was thinking of getting a whole new outfit anyway, lots of them, with belts and jackets for each outfit. Different from what I usually wear. More youthful, lower cut, that kind of stuff."

"Lower cut?" Pearl smirked. "What happened to your well-developed sense of prudery?"

"I don't know what it is," I said, "but the way I feel now, I can wear more feminine clothes." It had to be the gun; somehow, now that I felt safer, I could relax, be more open in public. "No more hiding my light under a bushel. Let the world see what a real woman looks like. I owe it to humanity."

"Okay, Norma," Pearl said, "you've had your big buildup. Now let's see the new you in your new they-should-all-drop-dead-from-envy opera gown."

"Oh my god, I forgot." All my evening gowns, the black one with the bolero and the same plain black one with the long-sleeved jacket instead of the bolero—which shows how much Alexander takes me out formal—were much too low cut to wear without anything on top, and much, much too old-fashioned for this kind of affair. The tall shops are okay for casual wear; I can get one size skirt and a larger blouse. But for a superelegant evening gown, the kind I had to have for the benefit—we were sitting in the boxes where only *rich* billionaires were allowed— I'd have to go to a superelegant couturier. Not only do they *never* have my size, they don't even have the patterns to make a gown that could be altered for me. I have to be draped and fitted, and that takes a long, long time. And costs like crazy. Not that we couldn't afford it now, but I still remember the days when Alexander quit his job to become a consulting engineer, and going over $19.98 was like breaking the sound barrier.

"As long as you have nothing to wear," Alexander said, "why don't we just stay home? I hate dressing up."

"It's for Tay-Sachs, Alexander. Genetic Diseases. We have to go. Pearl is vice-chairman and Julia Baron is in charge of the whole night. We can't leave any seats empty."

"So we'll give our tickets to some poor music students; let them have the big thrill. I already paid the thousand bucks per ticket, so Tay-Sachs won't lose. God, what a price for a lousy opera."

"We're sitting in the boxes, where everybody has to come formal. Poor students can't afford white-tie rentals. And don't complain, we can easily afford the money now, thank God. It's not the Pantheon Opera Company we're giving the money to, not *Rigoletto* we're paying for; it's charity."

"I already gave Tay-Sachs a huge donation a few months ago, or rather, Daniel Pereira Belmont gave it in my name. Come on, Norma, you know I hate opera; the plots are ridiculous, absolutely unbelievable."

"So why do you cry at every opera I've taken you to?"

"Brainwashing techniques, pure and simple. The loud music, the emotional content, the childish trickery. . .When I leave the opera house and can think clearly again, I see how silly it all is."

"Don't be stubborn, Alexander. I know you love *Rigoletto*."

"Only the music; the story is one of the stupidest. Can you imagine an assassin coming up to a guy in the street and asking if he wants anyone killed? Or a father not knowing he is kidnapping his own daughter out of his own house? And after Gilda has been stabbed in the heart, by a professional killer yet, and stuck in a sack, ten minutes later she sings the finale with Rigoletto. It's absolutely illogical." For Alexander, the ultimate insult.

"Can you also imagine, Alexander, Thea Malabar singing 'Caro Nome'? And Carlo Cacciare doing 'La Donna è Mobile'? Ettore D'Aquila as the hunchback? Plus Gregor Brezhnikov's first appearance since he defected? Even in a small role like Maddalena, you have Salome Auber. There'll never be a performance like this one, Alexander. Never in our lifetime."

"How is it that Brezhnikov is in this?" Alexander asked. "Shouldn't he be starring in *Boris Godunov* for his American debut?"

"He will," Pearl answered, "next month. But when Kerfiu died, and his cover singer had that terrible accident, Brezhnikov was the only major basso available for this production. I'm really sorry for the others, but I'm glad it happened this way; I just love those deep, rolling Russian bassos. We're lucky Kreuz was able to get him on such short notice."

"How did Thea Malabar allow a sexpot like Salome Auber to get into the cast?" I asked Pearl. "I thought she only allowed fat old ladies and raw beginners on the same stage with her."

"Kreuz must have persuaded her."

"Persuaded? From what I hear, nobody persuades Thea Malabar."

"What Pearl means," Burton explained, "is that Hugo Kreuz had a little talk with her. Remember when Rudolf Bing fired Maria Callas when she was at the height of her popularity? I met Kreuz once. Next to him, Bing is a Viennese cream puff."

"How did Kreuz get them all together in one production?" Alexander asked. "Don't they all hate each other?"

"They're professionals," Pearl said, confidently. "No one would do anything to spoil the performance. And they don't really hate each other, just some professional differences. Besides, contracts with major artists are made years in advance; they didn't necessarily hate each other then."

"Ettore D'Aquilla and Thea Malabar hate each other," Burton said. "I read about it today. Blood will flow in that performance."

"That's different," Pearl said. "They're married. It's only natural."

"Divorced," I corrected.

"Separated," Alexander recorrected. "They can't get divorced. He's Sicilian." Where he gets these odds and ends of information, I can't imagine; he never reads the gossip columns. "But it might be interesting to watch the real volcano underneath the fake fireworks on the stage."

"So don't be a pooper, Alexander," I said. "You'll love it. The last act of *Rigoletto* is the greatest blend of music, staging, and drama in all opera."

"Actually," Pearl said, "the third act of *La Bohème* is even better." The blonde doesn't know when to keep her mouth shut.

Alexander doesn't give in that easily; he likes to be coaxed. "What about that crazy Jan Valczyk, the boy genius? Isn't he going to do it in modern dress or something? Set in Detroit or Hoboken?"

Pearl always rises to the bait. "Certainly not, Alex. Jan Valczyk is really a very conservative traditionalist. He's just a little original in his staging and lighting. And sets. He's been very successful; always gets rave reviews, his whole team."

I had to change the subject; if Alexander got the idea that this was going to be modernistic, nothing could make him go. "How did you get a premier production with all these stars and Valczyk directing, Pearl? Don't benefits usually have 'charity casts'?"

"That was Julia Baron's idea. She felt we could arouse enough interest in this performance to double the price of the tickets. And it worked. We're making a bigger splash than Opening Night at the Met. Everybody will be there."

"We had to pay the Pantheon an extra hundred thousand to get *this* production," Burton said. "But I wrote a contract that tied them up like a mummy. If even *one* of the principals doesn't give a complete performance, the Pantheon loses half its fee. So we're definitely going to get what we're paying for."

"I read," I said, "that the rehearsals are closed and Valczyk is keeping everything a big secret. You have the inside, Pearl; what's the real lowdown?"

"All I can get, Norma, is dribs and drabs. Nobody knows anything. Or if they do, they don't dare tell. Valczyk swore that if even *one* of his surprises leaks out, he'll kill the performance. He means it too. And Kreuz says that if there is no performance, he'll sue everybody connected with the opera for everything they've got. And *he* means it too."

"Come on, Pearl," I urged. "You must know something."

"Well," she said reluctantly, "there haven't been any full-dress orchestra rehearsals yet; that will be done this week. There are only two full and one lighting rehearsals scheduled; everything else is piano rehearsals. The sets are being made outside and won't be in place until Monday; meanwhile they're working with chalk lines."

"But that's crazy," I said. "The singers will be falling all over themselves, bumping into each other, missing cues. It'll be like amateur night."

"Don't worry," Pearl reassured us. "Valczyk always works like this. To him, singers are stupid; wooden puppets who have to have every move choreographed for them. He gets very upset if things don't go as planned, very nasty, and the singers know it too. If they do exactly, but *exactly,* what he says, it will come out *exactly* the way he wants. He says."

"Is he going to mess up the music too?" Alexander asked.

"He wants nothing to do with the music," Pearl answered. "To quote him, 'If you close your eyes, everything you hear is Edelstein; if you close your ears, everything you see is Valczyk.' Edelstein says he loves it that way."

"So how is it, so far?" Alexander asked.

"The music is really great; Edelstein is doing his usual wonderful job. But I haven't seen one second of Valczyk's work. Even Julia Baron is barred from the rehearsals."

"I know someone who can't be kept out," Burton said slyly. "Minos Zacharias."

"That's where you're wrong, darling," Pearl said. "Everyone, but *everyone,* is barred."

"You mean even Thea Malabar doesn't have clout enough—?"

"Nobody has clout with Jan Valczyk. He once replaced the lead tenor a week before the opening of the Glyndebourne Festival, just for disagreeing with him during dress rehearsal. But I don't think Malabar wants Zacharias around anymore anyway. They are *definitely* not getting married."

"I don't blame her," I said. "A guy who killed his first wife might get in the habit."

"Come on, Norma," Pearl said. "He wasn't even on the yacht that night."

"Very convenient for him too," I said. "Men like Zacharias don't have to be there, you know; they just give orders."

"Wait a minute," Alexander said. "What's this about Thea Malabar marrying Minos Zacharias? If D'Aquilla won't, *can't* give her a divorce, how can she even *think* about getting married?"

"Obvious," I said, giving him a taste of his own medicine.

"After Zacharias had his own wife killed, Thea Malabar figured Zacharias would arrange a little accident for her husband. Then she and Zacharias could get married."

"Two murders?" Pearl was aghast. "Just to get married?"

"Maybe not on West 74th Street," I pointed out, "but billionaires are used to getting what they want when they want it."

"If that's the case," Pearl said, "why is Malabar hinting around that she won't marry Zacharias?"

"Maybe she's tired of his tomcatting around?" I suggested.

"In that crowd?" Pearl dismissed the idea.

"I thought this was the love affair of the century," Burton asked. "What makes you think they're not getting married?"

"My friends tell me"—Pearl looked around furtively, although we were the only ones in the house—"that Zacharias has been seen with Patricia Horgan in out-of-the-way restaurants."

"Now I know what it is," Burton said. "You're not the only one with secret sources." He smirked. "If you beg me—"

"Don't give him the satisfaction, Pearl," Alexander spoke quickly. "I'll tell you what it has to be."

"You?" I said. "What do you know about jet-set gossip?"

"Nothing," he replied. "But from what I deduced. . .Burton, the great mouthpiece, could only have heard that two unlikely sets of lawyers have been conferring. Given that Thea Malabar is on the outs with Minos Zacharias after all these years, even though his wife is no longer a barrier to their getting married; assuming that Patricia Horgan thinks she ought to get married again—it's been a year since she had a husband; her own, I mean—it has to be to someone equally famous, jet-setwise, and equally rich; and given, lastly, that the internationally notorious magnate is twenty years older than the internationally famous divorcée, then there will be an arranged marriage as soon as their respective attorneys work out a mutually satisfactory prenuptial contract. It was obvious."

Burton's mouth was open. We had seen Alexander complete patterns like this before, but it was still a surprise each time he did it. Alexander was so pleased I knew it was the right time to hit him. "So you *will* take me to the opera, darling," I said confidently.

He dragged his feet a little. "I'll have to buy a whole new outfit."

"We'll rent one," I told him, "because you're still losing weight." My word in God's ear. But until I got him below 200, I'd still have to worry about his damaged left ventricle. He hadn't taken a nitro pill for angina in a month, but that was no guarantee. "You'll look *so* handsome in tails, now that you're getting closer to your proper weight." Actually, he now looked like a *slightly* slimmer bald gorilla with glasses, but compared to when he was 240—gorgeous.

"I can't lose any more weight, Norma," he said. "I'm down to my absolute minimum now. My ribs are sticking out."

This I ignored; it was exactly what he said when he weighed 240, 230, 220, and 210. And what he would positively say when he hit 200. Little did he know that he was going to end up at 195. The charts said that a heavy-boned man should, at five foot six, weigh 165, tops. Given that he is—was—a power lifter—I told him I would break his knees if I caught him even *looking* at the heavy-lifting section in the gym—I'd let him have thirty pounds extra for muscle. That made his goal—*my* goal— 195, max. If he didn't hit that in three months, I'd have to take more drastic measures. Such as no food at all for a week. But meanwhile, no buying of clothes; it might give him the idea that I accepted his present weight as permanent.

"I'll go with you tomorrow and help you pick out a nice out-fit." There's not much choice in white tie and tails, but Alexander looks on anything that includes a tie as a non-masculine ordeal that requires a woman's approval. I don't mind. Actually, I enjoy dressing him up.

"I'll be ashamed of myself later, Norma," he said, "but all right. If you really want to go, I'll go too. But you have to get yourself a new dress. With either one of your black gowns"— he still thinks I have two—"and me in tails, we'll look like a pair of penguins."

So we were set. All I'd have to do is get a really terrific high-class evening gown, with a jacket and a belt strong enough to hold a holster, that would fit a six foot one lady with a Rubens-type build, in four shopping days.

Four days, huh? To produce the impossible gown? I'd show Alexander he wasn't the only one who could perform miracles with impossible deadlines. Watch and learn, buster; there's a few kicks left in the old girl yet.

3

"What a beautiful gown," Julia Baron gushed when we met in the lobby. "You look just like an Indian goddess. Is it real?"

"It's real, all right," I said, "but it isn't an 'it,' it's a 'them.' Two saris, sewn together to twice the length."

"But the width of the material, Norma? Indian women are so much shorter. A regular sari would come only to your knees."

"I didn't wind it around like a regular sari. What I did—"

"Wait," Julia interrupted. "I want Roberta to hear." She called her daughter, who looked absolutely gorgeous tonight: no glasses, and her long auburn hair plaited in a coronet high on her head. Now that she was loved, Roberta had stopped trying to look shorter. She was wearing proper heels and a slinky green gown that she must have ordered months ago, having even more trouble in the height department than I do, and being almost as big up front. With Roberta was, naturally, Lt. David Warshafsky, the stupid detective who was waiting to become as rich as her father, Max Baron, before he would propose. Fat chance, on a cop's salary. One of these days I'd have to have a talk with him.

"I bought two saris," I said, "exactly alike, dark red with gold thread borders, and sewed the short ends together to make a super-long sari. Instead of a petticoat, I'm wearing an old black skirt with my black bolero and a *very* low-cut bra. I added a wide belt to keep the whole thing from falling down, because I couldn't depend on the tucking in of the saris to hold the weight." What I didn't tell her was that the belt would also hold my belt holster. "Starting with the gold border of the sari at shoe level, Pearl wound the sari around me, and as she wound, she sewed the top of the sari to the gown. She kept winding, spiraling up the width of the border until I had one full turn around my waist. Then she made eight wide pleats, half facing left and half right, sewing them in place instead of tucking them in, facing each other. The outer two pleats were full length, the next two shorter, and so on, giving a drawn-drape effect, like a theater curtain. The remainder of the material I curled around my back and hung over my left shoulder. Voilà, instant evening gown; fits all sizes."

"It's very graceful, Norma," Julia said. "But you're so uncovered on top. What if the part over your shoulder billows out?"

"I'll make sure it won't. Tonight I'll move slowly and gracefully. I can't take long steps in this outfit anyway."

"It's very daring," Roberta said. "There'll be more people watching you than the opera."

"About time," I said. "Usually when I go out with Pearl I feel like the ugly chaperone." Pearl did look terrifically sexy, as always, but this time everybody was looking at me. And none of them knew I had a gun. The trick is misdirection. Keep their eyes focused on the big picture and they don't even think about the sneaky details.

"Jeffrey also did something clever." Julia was bursting with pride as she pushed her idiot son to center stage. "All by himself. Tell Norma and Pearl, Jeffrey."

"I sold the TV rights to this performance," Jeffrey said, "for plenty. Closed the deal at three o'clock today. Big fights with Kreuz and all the agents, but they finally bought my formula. Tay-Sachs gets a nice percentage."

"Great," Pearl said. She meant it too; it was time the Barons got a little *naches* out of their only son. "Does that mean there'll be special lights and TV crews in the way?"

"Valczyk wouldn't stand for that; that's part of what made the deal so hard. They'll have two fixed cameras in the back of the orchestra, one on each side, and two more, the same way, at the first balcony level."

"The film will come out pure black." I said it gently, not to upset him.

"It isn't film," Jeffrey said. "It's tape, so they can use image enhancing. And they're using the same type of lens as in *Barry Lyndon;* it can take movies by candlelight."

Well, if it worked, I'd give Jeffrey a gold star. But, knowing Jeffrey, I wasn't going to rush out and stock up on gold stars just yet; guaranteed he'd find a way to screw it up.

Alexander and Burton came back from mingling with the rich billionaires and we went to our box. As the biggest wheel, Julia Baron and her family had the center box; thanks to Pearl's good works, we were on the Barons' right. Burton's partners and their wives filled the other four chairs.

I moved my chair closer to Alexander's and took his hand. In spite of what he had said about opera, I knew he would enjoy the show. For once, everything was perfectly perfect; the trick is to make these moments last.

4

As the house lights dimmed, I noticed something strange. In front of every door in the opera house stood an usher holding a pole. At the top of the pole was a small black box with which the usher covered the exit light. "Is this legal?" I whispered to Alexander.

"I guess so," he whispered back. "They must have cleared it with the fire marshal, or the performance would have been stopped. If there's any trouble, the usher just drops the pole and the exit lights are visible again."

The theater was now completely dark. "How are the musicians going to see," I asked, "to play the overture?"

"Just watch." He shushed me. "Valczyk must have something up his sleeve."

We were kept in darkness for at least a minute. My eyes adjusted and began to pick up bits of light, little leaks from the exit sign boxes, threads of light under the curtain. Suddenly the curtain opened, very fast. It felt like an explosion of lightning to my wide-open pupils, but after a few seconds I could see that the lighting level on stage was very low. So low, in fact, that it looked absolutely natural: The ballroom of the sixteenth-century

Duke of Mantua, late afternoon western sunlight coming in through the tall, narrow windows on the right side of the stage, servants lighting candles on the darker, left side of the stage, just as they would in real life in such a room when the sun was beginning to set.

Valczyk had done something else that I just noticed—just noticed because it looked so right. Instead of the usual bare brown masonite, he had provided a real floor in the ballroom, and a ceiling too. The floor was inlaid marble, imitation, I'm sure; the ceiling was carved—or rather looked exactly like carved—painted plaster. The room was completely enclosed on three sides, no wings, no way to get in or out of the ballroom except for the double doors at the back and left side, and the corridor off the right rear. A *real* ballroom. The floor was slightly sloped down toward the auditorium and the ceiling sloped up a bit more so. To the singers it must have been like standing in a sound shell; guaranteed they would all sound great tonight. To heighten the reality, there were no footlights; no prompter's box.

In the ballroom, the courtiers and their ladies were slowly circulating, quietly talking to each other. Flirting, some laughter, occasional intelligible words—Italian, of course—a fancy dress cocktail party, overheard through a thin partition, seen from a distance. A small group of musicians in the far left corner of the ballroom, tuning up their instruments, looking bored. But still no music.

The western sun was setting, less and less light coming in through the windows at a lower and lower angle, light becoming tinged with pink, orange, red.

The fixed-bracket candelabra on the walls and the free-standing lamps were now all lit. Servants lowered the five huge chandeliers by their ropes and began lighting the dozens of candles on each fixture. As these lights grew brighter, I could see the faint glow, shielded from the audience by black enclosures, of the orchestra's tiny music lights snapping on, one by one, coordinated with the candles being lit on stage. Everything looked so real, so perfect, that, as the fully lit chandeliers were hoisted, in unison, back to the ceiling of the ballroom, the audience burst into applause. Even Alexander clapped. Jan Valczyk deserved it.

Edelstein, practically invisible from behind, his long black hair covering his white collar, lifted his baton and started the dark, brooding overture; a short prelude, really, a foreshadowing of the tragedy to come, of the curse, *La Maledizione,* that would be laid on the court jester, the doomed hunchback Rigoletto.

As the threatening overture ended, the opera began. The little band in the ballroom struck up a light gay melody. A courtier enters talking with the Duke, Carlo Cacciare, the handsomest man ever in opera. The audience exploded with applause and, I swear, there were women screaming, just as their mothers had screamed over Frankie when *they* were teenagers. And in front of their husbands too. No shame.

Cacciare, typecast as the libertine Duke of Mantua, did not have to step out of character to enjoy the screams but, typically, he milked the moment a little longer than even the world's greatest tenor should have. Edelstein finally gave the beat and the Duke sang, telling the courtier that he would soon be successful with the poor young girl he'd been meeting in church every day. The Duke followed the girl home regularly and saw an unknown man sneaking into the house every night.

The Duke catches sight of Countess Ceprano and remarks on her beauty. The courtier warns the Duke not to let Count Ceprano hear him, or the Count might tell the Duke's present mistress. This leads to the first great aria of the opera, "Questa o Quella" ("This Woman or That One," it doesn't matter). If one woman strikes the Duke's fancy today, he'll stop at nothing to get her, but tomorrow there'll be another. Again, great applause plus some screams, and again a hammy acknowledgment of what was, obviously, Cacciare's due as the world's greatest lover.

The band plays a little minuet. As they dance, the Duke flirts with Countess Ceprano and leads her out the back door to the next room. Count Ceprano has been watching jealously. The court jester, Rigoletto, enters. Although there are no screams, the applause for Ettore D'Aquilla, the great baritone, is as loud as for Cacciare. The hunchbacked Rigoletto asks the Count, insinuatingly, what is on his mind as he watches the Countess go off with the Duke, making sure everyone in the ballroom knows the Duke intends to seduce the Countess. Count Ceprano angrily follows the Duke and the Countess into the next room, as Rigoletto leaves by the left side door.

Another courtier enters, excited. He tells the others that he has discovered that the nasty, ugly dwarf, Rigoletto, has a mistress—a young girl he visits every night.

The Duke returns with Rigoletto, telling the jester how attractive he finds Countess Ceprano. Rigoletto slyly urges the Duke to take her. The Duke hesitates; her husband is in the way. Rigoletto viciously eggs on the Duke, suggesting jailing or even beheading the Count. The Count, overhearing this, draws his sword to kill Rigoletto, but as long as the jester is under the Duke's protection, the Count cannot harm his tormentor. Frustrated, Ceprano calls on the other courtiers, all of whom have felt Rigoletto's sharp tongue, to take revenge on the vicious dwarf. Angrily, the Duke warns Rigoletto that he goes too far. Turning to the courtiers, the Duke tries to revive the spirit of the party. The courtiers, who hate and fear Rigoletto, swear to have their revenge. Rigoletto taunts them, certain that he is safe.

As the ball starts again, it is interrupted by the entry of old

Count Monterone, who has come to challenge the Duke. Rigoletto sneers at the new victim, telling the old Count that it is futile to try to restore his daughter's honor. Monterone swears that he will avenge the insult to his house. He insists on facing the Duke, vowing he will have his say even if he is killed for it; that his ghost will carry on the vendetta.

Angered, the Duke orders the old Count's arrest. Monterone curses the Duke and turns on Rigoletto. For laughing at a father's pain, Monterone calls down a father's curse on the jester's head.

The last rays of the dying sun glow dimly through the windows, a blood-red beam outlining the vengeful Count and the terrified hunchback. It is getting dark. Half the candles have died, the rest are flickering wildly. The heavy music of doom rumbles louder, deadening the gaiety of the ballroom, mocking the jester's bright motley.

The angry Duke and his courtiers threaten Monterone, but the old Count stands proud and defiant, and again pronounces the curse on the Duke and Rigoletto.

Soldiers take the old man away and the courtiers depart, leaving the jester, frightened and trembling, alone in the red-black light, the sputtering candles making worm-shadows crawl over Rigoletto's face.

In the gathering darkness the hunchbacked dwarf crouches, twisted, stiff, one arm shielding his eyes, the other curled over his head, to ward off the terror, the curse, the relentless march of doom. The music rises, the last candle gasps out, the curtain falls.

5

Julia Baron was waiting impatiently outside my box. "Did you see it?" She gripped my arm. "Did you hear them?"

"The Duke and Rigoletto?" I asked.

"Carlo Cacciare and Ettore D'Aquilla," she corrected. "That was . . . Tell me what you feel, Norma."

"Well, I thought they—there seemed to be an undercurrent of antagonism there. But it might have been just acting, the way Valczyk told them to do it."

"That was for real," she said firmly. "But more than hate. There was fear too. And warning. When the Duke tells Rigoletto he is going too far, and Rigoletto smiles like no one can hurt him . . . I tell you, Norma, something bad is going to happen. I know."

I had had enough experience with Julia Baron to trust the fantastic accuracy of her predictions as well as her normal female instincts, but I wasn't exactly sure what she had in mind. "You mean," I said, "something bad is going to happen to Rigoletto? I thought he looked deathly afraid at the end of the act, but I put it down to the acting and the darkness."

"Blood," Julia said. "There will be blood. And D'Aquilla was frightened, but I don't know of what."

"Maybe of himself." Pearl had joined us. "He was born into a culture where the kind of passions we see only on the stage are part of the normal life."

"It can't be easy for him to be on the same stage with Thea Malabar," I pointed out. "In Sicily, the husband is supposed to kill the unfaithful wife and her lover."

"No one I know has ever seen Cacciare and Malabar together," Pearl said. "It's all gossip."

"When Cacciare is supposed to have slept with half the women in western civilization," I said, "and she brags she always has affairs with her leading men, you don't need a notarized affidavit."

"In Europe," Julia said, "it is not so terrible if it's the husband, but the wife must not only *be* pure, everybody must *believe* she is. What people think is more than what is real. Read the books, the papers, the murder trials."

"I am very knowledgeable about Italian literature," Pearl said. "It's part of my field."

"Not literature, Pearl darling," Julia said. "Read the magazines, the TV. That shows how people really feel."

Alexander came over to join us, and the conversation, at least the interesting part, stopped. Have you ever noticed how, with men around, we never talk about what's really important? Sometimes, like just now, I wish Alexander were like other men, the ones who hang together at parties discussing what they can't do anything about.

When we got back to our seats, the theater was completely dark again, and all I could see were green spots floating around in front of my eyes.

6

I wondered if Valczyk was going to continue his first-act technique of lighting the stage with what appeared to be natural light coming from the scene itself, and if he was, how he was going to do it. Moonlight on stage never looks real. The trouble is, I think, that directors and lighting experts feel they must show colors, and under real moonlight, everything is in black and white.

Valczyk's moonlight was real. It shone on the little house and its walled garden with spots of slowly moving darkness, the shadows of clouds gliding across the face of the moon. Again there was loud applause, quickly hushed as Rigoletto came walking down the ancient road, wrapped in a long cloak, shielding his face and looking around carefully to make sure he wasn't followed.

Rigoletto, still brooding about the old Count's curse, approaches the door in the garden wall. Sparafucile, the professional assassin who has been following Rigoletto unseen, appears and introduces himself as a man with a sword who, for a fee, will get rid of the rival Rigoletto has for the young lady he keeps locked up in the little house. Rigoletto is shocked into silence for a moment, then asks how much to kill a noble. A little more, Sparafucile tells him; half in advance, the rest after the murder.

Rigoletto asks for details. Sparafucile says that his pretty sister, a street dancer, entices the man into her inn. Once inside the house, Sparafucile stabs him. Sparafucile asks if his sword can serve Rigoletto, but the jester says not at this moment.

After Sparafucile leaves, Rigoletto sings the great aria "Pari Siamo" ("We Are Alike"): "I kill with my tongue, he kills with his sword." A soliloquy, really, a lament about his fate as a hunchback, a dwarf, a clown who must make his master laugh, no matter what. Rigoletto tells of his hatred of the courtiers and the pleasure he gets from tormenting them. His thoughts return again and again to the curse hanging over him as he goes through the door in the garden wall.

In the garden of his house, his beautiful blond sixteen-year-old daughter, Gilda, runs to greet him. He holds her tightly to him. Gilda asks about her dead mother, but Rigoletto puts her off. She asks why, although they moved here three months ago, they see no family or friends. Rigoletto tells her she is all he needs. He warns Gilda never to go out, and tells Gilda's nurse to watch over her, to make sure no one follows Gilda home from church. Hearing a noise, Rigoletto goes outside to look. Taking advantage of this, the Duke, disguised as a student, slips into the garden, throws the nurse a purse, and hides behind a tree. Rigoletto returns, warns the nurse not to let anyone in, says good-bye to his daughter, and leaves.

Gilda feels guilty about not telling her father about the handsome young man who follows her home from church every day. She tells her nurse that in her dreams she hears him say that he loves her. The Duke comes out from behind the tree and says, as if in continuation of her dream, that he loves Gilda. He sings his love for her, and the innocent young girl is swept off her feet.

Gilda asks her lover's name. The Duke gives a false name and, knowing this is what Gilda wants to hear, says he is a poor student. As they are swearing love for each other, the nurse rushes in. She has heard footsteps outside, and the Duke must leave at once.

Gilda climbs the stair to the balcony outside her bedroom and sings the beautiful coloratura aria "Caro Nome" ("Dear Name"), about her love for the poor student; not too well, I thought.

The noise the nurse heard was the gathering of the courtiers, bent on revenge, outside the house. They see Gilda on the balcony and remark on the beauty of Rigoletto's mistress.

Rigoletto returns to the dark street, still brooding about the curse. The courtiers tell him they are going to kidnap Countess Ceprano and invite him to join them. Using the excuse of masking him like the rest, they blindfold Rigoletto, turn him around so he doesn't know where he is, and make him hold the ladder while they climb the wall and enter Rigoletto's house, singing softly of the joke they are playing on the jester. They carry out Gilda, bound and gagged with her scarf. She manages to tear off the scarf and leave it behind, but Rigoletto does not hear her.

When Rigoletto realizes he is alone, he tears the blindfold from his eyes. He rushes into the house to find Gilda gone. He cries out her name, then realizes that the curse of Monterone has taken its first victim. Clutching the fallen scarf, he holds his heart as a cloud slowly darkens the scene.

7

This time I was waiting for Julia Baron at the door to her box. She was the first one out. As soon as she saw me, she grasped my arm and dragged me away from the others. "It is making me crazy," she said. "I saw it this time so clearly. Death is coming. Tell Alexander. He must not let this happen. You saw?"

"Sparafucile and Rigoletto?" I asked. "Brezhnikov is going to kill Cacciare? Hired by D'Aquilla?"

"No, no." She was impatient at my blindness. "Not hired. Brezhnikov is a singer, like D'Aquilla; he would not kill for salary."

"Then what? I was sure, at the beginning of the act, they were talking—singing—about really killing somebody. And when D'Aquilla asks how much to kill a noble, I just knew he meant Cacciare."

"Who I do not know yet. That is why Alexander must stop it."

"Alexander? How can he, Julia? He has no influence. Why not *your* husband? Max could stop the show, if anyone could."

"Norma, are you not understanding purposely? The show can

not be stopped. If Tay-Sachs must give all the money back, children will die."

"Then how?"

"Alexander is a famous detective now, and very easy to recognize. He must go in the back of the stage, tell everybody he is watching, so no funny business now."

I couldn't believe this. "Would *you* like to tell that to Alexander, Julia? He's still an engineer at heart; he'll never believe my feelings, or even yours. Without hard evidence—"

"He knows I am never wrong, Norma. Tell him. There will be blood on that stage unless . . . Please."

"We'll both tell him, Julia." I took her arm; we went over to where our husbands were standing, and Julia told them her fears.

"I really believe," Alexander said, "that you are an instinctive pattern maker, Julia. You integrate a large number of variables and predict the end result accurately. But this is not the case here. You have no information to work from; just feelings."

"My feelings are right, Alexander," she persisted. "Have you listened to how they sing? Even Gilda. There is not acting on that stage tonight. It is certain."

"Have you ever seen *Rigoletto?*" Alexander asked. "There is a murder in the last act, Julia. Is that what you're sensing?"

"I do not bother about *acting* murder." Julia's face was pale. "What I feel, it is real."

"What would it hurt, Alexander?" I said. "Do it for me."

That got him. I don't often ask, but when I do, Alexander will do anything I want, provided I don't try to justify it. He looked uncomfortable. "I can't just go backstage; they wouldn't let me in. And if I did get in, what would I do? Go around yelling, 'You better not kill anybody tonight; a watchbird is watching you'?"

"Pearl can get you in," I said. "Take Burton with you. He's a criminal lawyer. Just talk to each other about how you always get your man. Something like that. Loudly."

"It's too late," he said. "Intermission is almost over. Besides, nothing happens in the third act; no murder, I mean. I'll go during the next intermission. Okay, Julia?"

"I don't know," she said. "I hope you are right. But I do not think it will happen on the stage. Too many people are watching, and the TV cameras."

"Okay with you?" Alexander asked Burton. Burton nodded and smiled as though it would be fun. Not that I expected him to refuse. Max Baron, after all, was his firm's biggest client. "Who do I threaten, Julia?" Alexander asked, half smiling.

"Everybody," she said, not smiling. "Everybody."

8

The third act took us back to the ballroom of the Duke's palace. The Duke enters, shaken. He had returned to Rigoletto's house to find Gilda gone. Sure that she has been abducted, he is torn between rage that his next conquest has been taken from him and pity for the poor young girl.

The courtiers enter, laughing. They recount how, with Rigoletto's help, they have kidnapped his mistress. The Duke realizes what has happened, and goes off to find Gilda.

Rigoletto comes in, staggering and broken, trying to appear nonchalant. He walks around the ballroom, looking for signs of his daughter. The courtiers tease him. Rigoletto responds in his old sharp manner, and keeps on searching.

A page enters, looking for the Duke. The courtiers say he is hunting, cannot be disturbed. Rigoletto knows what this means: Gilda is with the Duke. The courtiers ask who Rigoletto is looking for. He says it is the girl they stole from his house, but that he will get her back. The courtiers joke, telling him that if he lost his mistress he should look elsewhere. Rigoletto, raging but still with dignity, sings the powerful words "Io Vó Mia Figlia" ("I Demand My Daughter").

The courtiers are shocked. Rigoletto runs to the door of the Duke's rooms. The courtiers bar his way. He sings the great aria "Cortigiani, Vil Razza" ("Courtiers, Vile Race"), as he tries to force his way into the Duke's rooms. Again the courtiers stop him.

Gilda comes out of the Duke's rooms and confesses her shame to her father. Rigoletto orders the courtiers out, and says that the Duke himself had better not come in. Gilda tells Rigoletto the story of her love and her betrayal. Rigoletto tells his daughter that it is all right to weep, that he will take her away from Mantua.

The candles are burning low, going out, as two guards lead old Count Monterone across the back of the room to the dungeons. Monterone stops before the Duke's portrait, regretting that his curse has not destroyed the Duke. Rigoletto tells the old man that he will be avenged. The room slowly darkens and the music grows louder. Facing the Duke's portrait, Rigoletto swears vengeance: "The Clown Knows How to Strike Like Lightning." Gilda quietly sings to herself that she still loves the Duke. She begs Rigoletto to forgive. Rigoletto refuses, and sings of his revenge even more loudly and violently. The stage goes dark as the curtain comes down on Rigoletto's rage and Gilda's tearful pleading.

9

Julia Baron practically pushed Alexander, Burton, and Pearl toward the stairs. "Make sure to talk loud," she ordered. "All over."

"Why all over?" I asked. "It's obvious to me that D'Aquilla is going to get his revenge. Did you hear how he sang 'Vendetta! Vendetta!'? He meant it, Julia; he was enjoying it. And when Gilda sang 'Perdonate' ('Forgive Him'), the way he said, 'No!' they weren't talking about the Duke of Mantua; they meant Carlo Cacciare."

"Of course they did," Julia said impatiently. "You don't need two eyes to see that Cacciare and Malabar are having a big affair. He always does and she always does."

"So why did you tell Alexander to go all over? A quiet talk with D'Aquilla—"

"You Americans. Even you, Norma, you think everything is like Hollywood? Punch *him* in the nose, kiss *her,* everything is okay, happy ever afterwards? No. In Europe it is different. Honor is important, especially by the Mediterranean. Sicily—you kill the wife *and* the lover. Then you are a man again, not a cuckoo. You understand?"

"But this is America, Julia. We don't do that here."

"*You* don't, maybe. D'Aquilla? I don't know. And what about Minos Zacharias? Crete is more south than Sicily. And Cacciare? You think he is going to sit still? Wait for having his throat cut? Maybe he will kill first."

"But Brezhnikov, Julia. He's here only a few months. Why him?"

"I don't know why. But much can happen in a few months. You heard him sing 'Only a little more for killing a noble.' You think he means the president? No. He is Russian. Very serious. No jokes."

"Then wouldn't it be better to have one of the security men guard Thea Malabar?"

"Guard for what? Someone to kill her? You think *she* cannot kill? Ha! She is more than the men."

"But she's American, Julia. From Pennsylvania."

"American from Pennsylvania, Norma? That means guarantee not to kill? I think, Norma"—Julia shook her head—"you do not like to believe what you see, what you hear. Alexander, my Max, they would trust only a lie detector machine, but you are a woman, Norma."

"All right, Julia." I gave in. "But, really, what can be done? These people are opera singers, Julia, artists. They're all a little unstable, and they're all keyed up for tonight. Granted. But if Alexander stops them tonight, what about tomorrow? Or next week? We can't watch them all forever."

"For next week I don't care, Norma. I just don't want scandal tonight. It would be a bad public relations for Tay-Sachs. Tay-Sachs is very important, Norma. No one will spoil it if I can help."

The bell tones sounded. Alexander wasn't back yet. I went into our box, concentrating on not letting anything bad happen. It never worked before, but who knows?

10

"**I** felt like an idiot," Alexander said. "But Burton really enjoyed it."

"Did you cover the whole backstage area?" I asked. "The way Julia said?"

"Twice. I really put the fear of God into two stagehands and a dresser."

In this mood, there was no sense talking to him. Anyway, the curtain was going up.

On the left, a dark, dilapidated old inn, its rough wooden floor two steps above stage level, cracked planks on the side of the house. On the right, the bank of a river, real water, black, lapping the stones. Threatening storm clouds coming closer. Twilight turning into night.

Maddalena, carrying a candle, enters the big downstairs room of the inn from an arch at the left. She fixes the candle to a long holder and lights the candles in the wall brackets on the outside wall of the house, high up, one by one. As each candle is lit, the interior of the inn gets lighter and lighter; the planks making up the side of the house, which were painted on the scrim, disappear as the inside brightens. A cloud blocks the moonlight and, as the outside gets darker, the inside becomes clearly visible. A line of rough-adzed posts down the middle of the big room supports the plank-and-beam second floor. A big stone fireplace in the rear wall, near the entrance to the inn, gives a soft glow to the room; the embers occasionally burst into small flames. Along the back wall, to the left of the fireplace, the open wooden stair leads leftward up to the second floor of the inn.

Sparafucile enters the downstairs room from the dark arch at the left, sits at a table, and starts polishing his sword belt.

The storm clouds sliding across the face of the rising moon make slowly moving shadows on the road at the side of the inn, which leads from left to right and, making a left turn past the inn's entrance, continues parallel to the river to the back of the stage.

The cloud over the moon passes as Rigoletto and Gilda enter from the left, along the road, turn, and stand facing the transparent side of the inn, their backs to the audience. Rigoletto asks Gilda if, after a month, she still loves the Duke. She admits she will love him forever and begs her father to have pity on the Duke. Rigoletto asks what she would say if there were proof the Duke had betrayed her. Innocent Gilda is sure the Duke still loves her.

Rigoletto leads her closer to the inn to look through the cracks in its wall. Inside, the candles are all lit and it is easy to see the Duke, disguised as a cavalier, enter through the front door. He orders a room and wine, and, as Sparafucile leaves through the dark arch at the left, the Duke sings "La Donna è Mobile" ("Women Are Changeable").

Sparafucile returns with the wine and two glasses, and taps on the ceiling with his sword. Maddalena, his sister, comes down the stair. The Duke tries to kiss her as Sparafucile goes out the front door to talk to Rigoletto. "Does he live or die?" he asks Rigoletto. "I'll let you know soon," Rigoletto answers.

As Gilda watches through the cracked planks, the Duke makes advances to Maddalena and even proposes marriage. "Have you had enough?" Rigoletto asks his daughter. Gilda is hurt and angry. The Duke, Maddalena, Gilda, and Rigoletto sing the famous quartet, each following his own thoughts: Maddalena leading the Duke on; the Duke wooing Maddalena; Gilda realizing these are the very words the Duke spoke to her; Rigoletto swearing he will kill the Duke and avenge the insult.

Rigoletto tells Gilda to go home, disguise herself as a boy, get a horse, and go to Verona, where he will soon meet her. After Gilda leaves, Sparafucile approaches Rigoletto again. Rigoletto gives him ten gold pieces, half the fee in advance for the murder. Sparafucile asks who the victim is. Rigoletto replies, "His name is Crime and my name is Punishment."

Sparafucile goes back into the inn and tells the Duke that the storm is almost upon them. The Duke says he will spend the night. Maddalena, who has fallen in love with the Duke, tells him he must not stay. Sparafucile reminds his sister of the twenty gold pieces. The Duke takes a single candle upstairs, softly sings a bit of "La Donna è Mobile," lies down on the bed, blows out the candle, and falls asleep.

Gilda appears, dressed in men's clothing, lovelorn and confused. She overhears Maddalena begging Sparafucile to spare the Duke, suggesting that her brother kill the hunchback instead and take his money then. Sparafucile refuses; as a man of honor he must keep his bargain. Finally, after Maddalena's continued pleading, Sparafucile agrees that if anyone else comes to the inn before midnight, he will kill the stranger instead. Maddalena objects: It is late, the storm is upon them, no one will come. A clock strikes.

As the storm grows fiercer, Gilda decides to sacrifice herself for the man she still loves. She knocks on the door. Sparafucile says it is the wind. The storm grows fiercer, louder. Gilda knocks again, harder. Sparafucile gets his dagger. Gilda knocks a third time. Sparafucile stands behind the door, the raised dagger in his right hand catching a flash of candle flicker. Maddalena opens the door. Gilda steps in. Maddalena throws a cloth over Gilda's head as Sparafucile stabs her in the heart. Gilda screams and falls to the floor. Maddalena holds a sack and helps Sparafucile stuff Gilda's limp body inside, leaving only her head, with its long golden hair, visible. He drags the sack away from the entrance and leans it against the post in the middle of the room, propping Gilda's head against the post. Her head drops forward, the golden hair cascading down the front of the sack.

Sparafucile takes a candle and goes out through the dark arch at the left side of the room. Maddalena takes a long candle snuffer and puts out the candles in the room, leaving only the one on the outside wall opposite Gilda's body. She takes a candle and stands in front of Gilda's body, bends forward and checks the sack, then goes to the stair. Halfway up she stops for a moment, then continues her climb. She goes into the Duke's room. They embrace and he blows the candle out.

Sparafucile returns with a glass of wine and sits at the fireplace, facing the front door, waiting for Rigoletto to return with his money.

Rigoletto comes back on the road, chewing at the revenge he has been waiting for. The night has darkened with the storm, making Gilda's body visible through the scrim. Her long golden hair picks up the candle's gleam, mocking her father's victory.

The church clock strikes midnight. Rigoletto knocks at the door of the inn. Sparafucile pushes Gilda's head into the sack, knots the cord around the end, and drags the grisly bundle out to Rigoletto. Rigoletto pays the assassin. Sparafucile offers to throw the sack into the river, but Rigoletto wants to complete his revenge himself. He starts dragging the sack toward the river, when he hears the Duke singing "La Donna è Mobile."

Stunned, Rigoletto cuts open the sack with his dagger. A flash of lightning reveals Gilda's head. He screams, runs to the inn, beats on the door. All is silent.

The music for the final duet between Gilda and Rigoletto begins, the one Alexander thought was so silly, but Gilda does not sing. Here Valczyk's genius showed again. The missing voice, as Rigoletto sang the closing duet himself, grief-stricken, was so much more poignant than Gilda's usual tweeting about meeting her mother in heaven, that I, and I *never* do it, even I found myself crying for the poor broken hunchback, the father of the dead little girl, the accursed Rigoletto.

As the music rose to its final crescendo, Rigoletto screams "La Maledizione" ("The Curse") and collapses next to Gilda's body. The curtain came down and the audience exploded, screaming applause, bravos, with a few boos from, I am sure, Thea Malabar's claque.

Suddenly Alexander got up, pushed past Burton, and *ran* out of the box.

11

L t. David Warshafsky, standing next to the body and looking completely wrong in white tie without his dinner
jacket, was trying to get things organized. "Everybody get the
hell off the stage," he yelled, waving his badge wallet. "And
nobody leaves the backstage area." He caught sight of me. "Call
Homicide, Norma," he yelled. "I need help fast."

I motioned to Pearl to do it and ran to Alexander. "Nitro?" I
asked.

He was standing perfectly still, breathing deeply and evenly.
"Took one already," he said. "I'm okay."

"You're not supposed to run, you moron." I held him tightly.
"What are you trying to do, kill me?"

"I just wanted . . . I don't know. See if I could find anything
before the stagehands took the set apart."

"Why, Alexander?" I asked. "We're not involved. We don't
have a client. Warshafsky is here; let the police handle it."

He looked at me as though I was crazy. "Right in front of my
eyes and we're not involved? I could have stopped it if I had
paid attention to Julia. I should have realized, when she didn't
sing—"

"You did everything you could, Alexander, everything Julia wanted. What else could you have done, stopped the show in the middle? That's just what Julia didn't want."

Burton came over. "She's right, Alex. There was no way for us to do anything. I don't think the publicity will hurt Tay-Sachs at all; it's clear they had nothing to do with this."

"Will we have to give any money back?" Pearl had returned from phoning the police.

"Certainly not," Burton said. "Everybody saw the whole show except for five minutes of Thea Malabar. And they loved it. As a matter of fact, I might even get some extra money for Tay-Sachs. Remember the clause I told you about? That every principal had to give a full performance? Hugo Kreuz will turn blue."

"I want everyone to stand still," Warshafsky yelled. "Stay where you are. Anyone who leaves the backstage area will have a hell of a lot of explaining to do."

Max Baron came in with Hugo Kreuz, the cold-eyed managing director of the Pantheon Opera. Two steps behind—I recognized him from his pictures—was Jan Valczyk, like Kreuz in white tie and tails. Typically, Baron had analyzed the situation and had done what was best under the circumstances.

"Mr. Baron has told us who you are, Lieutenant," Kreuz said in a heavy German accent, "so there is no need for wasting time. We place at your disposal our security forces." Kreuz nodded at the beefy man who had just come up. "This is Captain Morgan, our chief of security." Morgan looked just like one of the rich billionaires in his white tie outfit. I guess when you're mingling with potential murderers, you have to blend in. Half the people backstage were wearing white tie; prepared to take their bows, presumably.

"Good. Thanks." Warshafsky looked a bit less harried. "Glad you're here, Captain. I'd like you to keep everybody away from the body or any part of the set. Don't let anybody leave, or dispose of anything, or . . . Hell, you're an ex-cop, aren't you, Morgan?" The big man nodded. "Then you know what to do."

"Is there anything else you require, Lieutenant?" The skin on Kreuz's brutal face was pulled tight. "I have many things to do, under the circumstances."

"I realize that, Mr. Kreuz," Warshafsky said, "but there's been a homicide."

"You are sure?" Kreuz asked. "Performing an opera is a great stress. Some artists have died on stage, you know."

"You want me to take my jacket off her, Mr. Kreuz?" Warshafsky looked ready to blow up.

Kreuz shook his head slightly. "Not necessary; you are the professional. But I would like the report of the medical examiner. For our insurance carrier, you know. Is there any other way I may be of service, Lieutenant?"

"When the technical crew gets here, I'd like somebody with clout to go around with them to make sure they go wherever they want without any problems. I'll need a room, too, where I can question the witnesses in privacy."

"These are world-famous artists, Lieutenant," Kreuz demurred. "They cannot be treated like ordinary, uh, people."

"I can always take them down to the station." Warshafsky looked Kreuz straight in the eye.

"It shall be as you wish, Lieutenant." Kreuz could have made a good living as an actor, typecast as the martinet U-boat commander.

Which reminded me. "The movies, David," I said. He looked at me blankly. "What Jeffrey arranged. The TV cameras. They took pictures of everything."

He slapped his forehead. "Hell, yes. With all this . . ." He looked around. Captain Morgan was coming back. "One more thing, Morgan. Can you get a man to the TV crews? Tell them I want those tapes under police seal. If one bit of tape is wiped, I will personally tear the arm off—"

"Take it easy, Lieutenant," Morgan said. "I put a man with each crew for good luck. I already talked to them, walkie-talkie. Everything's under control."

"Thanks, Morgan, it's a relief to have a pro here."

"What I came in for—your people will be here in a couple of minutes. I told my guys to turn over jurisdiction as soon as your crew takes over, but to hang around, just in case. We know where everything is; your guys don't."

"Thanks, Morgan. We'll be in for a long night, taking statements."

"We also make good coffee." He hesitated. "You didn't tell me not to let the audience go, Lieutenant. There are some pretty big wheels here tonight and . . . No way to keep them, but I had some doors out of order, so that slowed things up a bit. Okay with you?"

"Fine, Morgan, just fine."

"I also had a couple of guys at each exit to make sure none of the employees walked."

"All I want is the people who were backstage during the last act."

"Takes an awful lot of people to make an opera, Lieutenant."

"I know," Warshafsky said wearily, looking at the hours of interviews ahead. "I guess I'm just lucky." He turned to us. "You're audience too. Go home."

"But, David," Alexander said, "I'll be happy to—"

"Later," David said. "First I have to do the horsework, and then I have to mess up the case. After that you can play detective." He sounded a little bitter. I didn't really blame him. It's hard to do anything right with a genius around. I know.

12

I had made broiled kippers for breakfast, Alexander's favorite, but it didn't help. "Did you hear what Warshafsky said?" Alexander was still boiling from last night. "You're audience too, he says. Go home. After all I've done for him?"

"He had to interview the witnesses, Alexander," I said.

"I'm not a witness?"

"You and two thousand others. Wouldn't *you* have interviewed the backstage people first?"

"But I'm a professional, Norma. I could have seen what nobody else saw."

"So what did you see, professional, that nobody else saw?"

"I was too involved in the opera; like you, Norma. But Warshafsky couldn't have known that until he asked me. And wasn't I the first to realize Thea Malabar had been murdered? Right in front of everybody's eyes?"

"*Mazeltov,* Alexander; another gold star. How long after she was killed did it take you?" It slipped out before I could think. The fastest lip on the West Side strikes again.

Surprisingly, he didn't blow up. "I'll give you the timetable after I solve the case."

"What case?" The quicker I digressed, the better. "Warshafsky can't hire you, especially at what you've been charging lately."

"Kreuz can," he said. "Or Tay-Sachs. Max Baron; he knows what I can do."

"Why should Kreuz care who did it?" I said. "Or Tay-Sachs? Or anyone else? Face it, Alexander, nobody's going to pay you to find the murderer."

"Then I'll do it on my own," he said. "You think I'm going to let that arrogant bastard commit murder while I'm watching and get away with it?"

"Whoever he was, Alexander, he didn't know you were watching. But I'll tell you what I'll do. I'll put a big ad in the papers: 'Whoever killed Thea Malabar, please call Alexander Magnus Gold collect, and explain that you didn't do it just to irritate him.'"

"I'm *involved* in a problem and you want me *NOT TO SOLVE IT?*" He sounded like I was asking him to betray Earth to the Aliens from Outer Space.

"Sorry, darling, I wasn't trying to talk dirty. All I meant was that you were one of two thousand people who might have seen a murder committed. That doesn't mean you're personally involved and have to dedicate the rest of your days to bringing the evil perpetrator to justice. And I, especially, as a licensed professional private investigator, will not do any licensed professional private investigating unless I have a paying client."

"It's my civic duty," he said, trying to look like an Eagle Scout. Oh, God, when Alexander starts talking that way . . . He positively *knows* that governments are the source of one hundred and three percent of all the evil in this world, and if we only had pure classic anarchy . . . Or, failing that, if Alexander Magnus Gold were elected Dictator of the Universe . . . I was saved, barely, from a lecture on the overly liberal failings of Adam Smith by the ringing of our other phone.

This was my new direct extension from A. I. Kaplan, Inc., the detective agency in which Pearl and I were the majority partners. As soon as we had transferred the stock, Art Kaplan, shadower *extraordinaire,* had cut expenses by firing his secretary, the non-hard-drinking, tired, and cynical, buxom blonde, *Mrs.* Art Kaplan, and had installed an extension, along with a phone-answering machine, in my house. I didn't mind, actually; it was very convenient: I didn't have to go to the office downtown unless I wanted to. Pearl, of course, loved the phone; it made her feel like a we-never-sleep guardian of the peace.

"A.I.K.," I said politely, although the last thing I wanted was for Alexander to take on the opera murder case. But you think God cares what I want?

The voice was cultivated British, well above upper-upper. And definitely phony. I mean, nobody out of Debrett's is going to be a low-level, or even a mid-level, working girl placing phone calls in New York this early in the morning. "This is the office of Minos Enterprises," she said, "calling Alexander Magnus Gold."

I don't like being held on "hold" while some big shot checks his watch to make sure I've been properly put down; I don't like phony accents, even British; I certainly didn't want Alexander to take a case right now, especially one that looked this frustrating; and I definitely was not in the mood to get involved with a guy who, in spite of what Pearl said, had probably killed his wife (who needs to give the filthy little beasts any *more* ideas?). I flipped on the speaker so Alexander could hear, but motioned him to keep his mouth shut on pain of frozen TV dinners. "I'm sorry," I said, "Mr. Gold does not talk to offices. Please have a human being call." I could have been less polite, but I didn't want Alexander to get a heart attack either, from frustration at not being able to bring himself to strangle me.

This stopped the Queen's Lady-in-Waiting for a while; I guess she had spent so much energy on the accent, she didn't have enough oxygen left for thinking. "This *is* a human being," she said, sounding miffed. "Please put Mr. Gold on."

Minos Zacharias, the Bull of the Bourse—what other Minos could it be?—playing the one-up game? How could a zillionaire be that insecure? And immature? Men!

Nobody beats Norma Gold at that kind of crap; *nobody.* "Deposit another nickel, please," I said sweetly, and hung up.

Before Alexander could scream, I explained. "She was ordered to get you on the phone. She'll call back, guaranteed. Let me handle this." He stuck out his lower lip, but sulking I can live with. The question was, Do I play it so hard it becomes impossible for Zacharias to retain Alexander, giving Alexander a heart attack from frustration? And, knowing him, he'd probably try to solve the case *without* a client, for which we'd get paid zilch *minus* expenses even if he solved it. Or should I take the case and give Alexander a heart attack from frustration if he couldn't solve it, and this looked exactly like one of *those* cases. Just because he'd been lucky so far . . . As usual, thanks to my dear husband's idiot peculiarities, I was in a position where whatever I did was wrong. To hell with it. I'd do what came naturally; there were no lines to remember that way.

The phone rang again. I picked up but didn't say a word. After a few seconds the same voice said, "Hello? We were cut off. This is the office of Minos Enterprises calling."

"Have whoever wants to talk to Mr. Gold place the call." I hung up again.

"Do you realize"—Alexander was at slow simmer—"that he wants to retain me? To find the murderer?"

"That's obvious," I said. It feels good for *me* to say it once in a while.

"Then why are you trying to drive him away? Don't you want me to have a client?"

I sidestepped that question. "Anything your little heart desires, sweetie. But getting the guy by playing hard to get is one of the many things women are better at than anybody else. Besides, *you* can't have clients for crime-solving, remember? Only a licensed P.I. can, and that's me. So kindly shut up or *I* won't retain you as a consultant when I hook Minos Zacharias for you, completely against my better judgment."

He looked smug. "You can't solve a murder like this without me. Nobody can." At least his lower lip was back in place.

"I don't have to take the case in the first place, either. It won't kill *me* if I never find out who killed Thea Malabar." I was bluffing, of course; Alexander was within two hours of having the top of his head blow off.

"Pearl will take the case if I ask her. She understands."

"She also understands what happens to her if she crosses me," I pointed out. But enough "teasing the animals" time; I've learned to gauge Alexander's limits, and this was it. "I didn't say I wouldn't take the case. As a special favor to you, I will. Under two conditions. Three."

"What?" he asked suspiciously.

"One, no more running." He nodded. "Two, you owe me a big one." He nodded again, less enthusiastically. "And three, you let me handle Zacharias in my own way."

He thought this over for a moment. "Okay," he said. "But if you lose Zacharias as a client, you owe me a big one *and* you have to get me another client. For *this* murder."

Before I could agree, thank God—no way was I ever going to lose a bet to Alexander; I *needed* him owing me—the phone rang again. I picked up and said nothing again. It took her ten seconds to see that she would have to speak first. "This is Mr. Zacharias' personal aide. May I speak to Mr. Gold?" This time the voice was human, mature, confident.

"What do you want to talk to him about?" I asked.

"Mr. Zacharias would like to speak to Mr. Gold," she said.

"So who's stopping him?" I hung up. Alexander began to go into labor. I leaned over and stroked his forehead. "Within ten minutes," I assured him, "tops. Guaranteed."

There must have been a heavy conference going on, deciding the fateful question: Would Minos Zacharias actually place a call *himself*? In person? With his own hot little hands? It was evidently decided *he* would, although it took him over five minutes to steel himself to the task. "Mr. Gold, please," he said, in a soft voice with a slight British accent.

"Who's calling, please?" The time to twist the knife is when you've got him down.

There was some heavy breathing of the wrong kind, so I switched on the recorder; I've always wanted to learn classical Cretan curses. He fooled me. "I am Zacharias," he said. "I wish to discuss retaining Alexander Gold to perform some services for me."

"I'm sorry, Mr. Zacharias," I said. "Mr. Gold cannot do anything for you directly. He has a lifetime contract with me." In my book, a marriage is for life, right?

"Ah, then you are Mrs. Gold." At least he wasn't stupid. "Good. I'll see Mr. Gold, and you too, of course, here at nine o'clock exactly."

Trying to get into the dominant position again? Not with Norma Gold, undisputed ploymaster of West 74th St. "Make that exactly eleven, here," I said. "If you're late, just sit on the stoop and wait for us. We should be back in an hour or two." I hung up and switched on the answering machine. Although I waited, the phone didn't ring again. I didn't really think Minos Zacharias was a yo-yo, but it doesn't hurt to check.

"You took an awful chance, Norma," Alexander said. "What if he decided not to call back? You know I'd still go ahead and solve the murder, and we wouldn't get a penny for it."

"If it gives you pleasure to get frustrated and irritated, and to risk Pearl's life, it's okay; we can afford not to get paid. A man your age needs a hobby anyhow. But when his secretary's receptionist called, at eight A.M. yet, I knew he had fixed on you. The rest was to ensure that he would pay, pay well, and pay promptly. So let me handle the business today."

"He may complain to Max Baron about the way you treated him. I don't want to hurt Max's feelings."

"Neither do I; he's a good guy. But Max didn't exactly recommend Zacharias to you, you'll notice; he recommended you to him."

"Granted; otherwise he would have given Zacharias our home phone. Do you think our new client has enough clout to get me the police data?"

"All billionaires have enough clout to get anything. Almost. But since New York is not his home base, he may not be able to work fast enough. I'll make it part of the deal that he—no, we—retain Burton to do our local bureaucratic expediting. He's highly respected and has enough contacts to get practically anything you need."

"Then shouldn't we have Burt here? To handle the contract and to hear what Zacharias has to say?"

"I was just going to call him over. Pearl too. I have some horsework for her to do, researching Zacharias."

"What if Burt has appointments scheduled?"

"Can you see Burton giving up a chance to meet another billionaire? And to joust with his attorneys?"

"I guess not. But please don't needle Burt too much; we really need his contacts with the police and the D.A.'s office. Warshafsky didn't sound too cooperative last night."

"That was last night. How would you sound if you were looking forward to going home with an acre of sexpot like Roberta Baron and instead you had to stay up all night talking to opera singers? He'll come around."

"I hope you're right. Before . . . what you said . . . You're going to negotiate *my* fee?"

"Absolutely. Today I do all the talking. You didn't want to be a licensed P.I., remember? So A.I.K. negotiates the price, which includes your consulting fee. If you're nice for a week straight, I might even pay you part of what I collect."

Even though I smiled when I said that, I could see he didn't like the idea. Not the part about getting paid—I handle all the money in the family anyway—but the part about negotiating his fee. But what could he do? He had made his choice at the time of the Belmont case, and there was no way he was going to show me he regretted the decision. It's good it worked out this way; it gave me another chance to change my mind about Alexander's taking the case. Maybe I'd set such terms and conditions that any self-respecting billionaire would tell me to shove myself and walk out. Whereupon Alexander might blame Zacharias for not hiring him instead of blaming me. Then again, he might not.

13

One of the disadvantages of our new computer is the lack of personal contact; I miss gabbing with researchers, reporters, and librarians. Also, from a computer you don't get a Norma Gold–type report, brilliantly written, all the facts in order, important data highlighted, and put together with love. On the other hand, no one can deny it's the best way to get data and information fast, especially if you're plugged into all the major data bases. It's simple too; even Pearl can use it.

Halfway through the printouts—stacks and stacks; Zacharias was not one to hide his light under a bushel—I sent Pearl home to change. Pearl would give Minos Zacharias what, I had discovered, he liked, while I gave him the business. I also gave Burton detailed instructions. Based on what I had learned so far, I thought I knew how to handle Mr. Z. All three of us would have a busy time of it; I just hoped Alexander would be able to keep his big mouth shut; in dealing with billionaires I needed all the help I could get. It was not an idle worry; Pearl and Burton would do what I said, but Alexander had a whim of iron.

The bell rang at one minute after eleven. Minos was still trying, but he had lost, and he had to know I knew he had lost.

That one-minute-late business didn't change things, but just to keep him in his place, I didn't buzz the front door until he rang a third time. That would teach him to start up with me. I hoped.

Pearl looked absolutely gorgeous, in a blond sort of way: low-cut white blouse, light blue skirt, demurely short, and stockings, not pantyhose. Her long golden hair was pulled back, tied with a red silk scarf, and flung over her right shoulder. Zacharias didn't even notice me as I introduced him to Alexander and Burton. I had deliberately dressed in a dark business suit, Burton in lawyer drab, and Alexander in slacks and polo shirt. They had both balked at the masquerade, but Pearl was on my side, so they were helpless. Burton especially I had ordered to say nothing unless I asked him a direct legal question.

Minos Zacharias was taller than his photos made him appear, at least five foot nine, but so broad at the shoulders that he could have worn Alexander's jacket. Zacharias' hips were so slim, and his feet so tiny, that his nickname might have come as much from his bull-like proportions as from his dealings in the stock market. His head was disproportionately large, covered with small, tight gray curls. From his thrust-forward nostrils and the knobby protrusions on his forehead, I could easily believe that he had once been a satyr in ancient Crete. And still was, if my computer printout was even one percent accurate.

Zacharias was burning to start talking business, so I played hostess, pressing him to have some coffee and Danish until he accepted. "What kind of coffee," I asked, "instant or Turkish?"

That really caught his attention. "It is not necessary, Mrs. Gold," he said, "to continue playing this childish game."

"You started," I said.

"I don't think you realize," he said, "but you have caused me difficulties within my organization which will take me weeks to repair."

"The Duchess of Wellington and our next Secretary of State?"

He sighed. "They've been with me for years, old and valued assistants who are very good at their work."

"Which is to one-up anyone who calls?"

"Among other things, yes. In my . . ." He stopped and seemed to be debating with himself. "Billionaires are different from other people."

"They're richer?"

"That's an old joke." He brushed it aside. He took a deep breath and spoke in a different tone of voice, almost lecturing. "Billionaires don't *have* money, except for some Arab misers; billionaires *control* money. They direct it, channel it, valve it. Nobody lives long enough to put a penny a day in the bank and let it slowly grow to a billion dollars. You must have the accumulated capital; the savings of many people, concentrated in institutions, banks, and the like. These institutions create money, more money than is given to them as savings. This new money must be given out, put out to work, to provide a return to the investors, depositors, savers. So the banks lend the money, provide the money, to people, companies, they believe will give them a good return, a secure return. Who gets the money, Mrs. Gold?"

"People who have lots of money already? People who don't need money?"

"Not quite right, Mrs. Gold. People who don't need money, don't borrow. And there was a time, long ago, when I was able to borrow money, huge sums of money, when I not only did not have any money, but was deeply in debt. So how was it done, Mrs. Gold?"

"They *thought* you had money."

"Precisely, Mrs. Gold. And why did they think that?"

"They thought you were a billionaire. Your yacht, your homes, your starlets, your life-style."

"Part of which, Mrs. Gold, is that when I wish to speak with someone, that person waits for *me,* in my reception room, or on the phone, until I am ready for him. Otherwise, the illusion begins crumbling at the edges, and one day, crack, it disappears. And that day, you may be sure—the gods have a sense of humor—that day is the day I need money desperately, to save my life."

"But you are a billionaire now, aren't you?"

He smiled. "How do you know, Mrs. Gold? Did I not speak first, to the secretary of a little-known detective? Did I not go to the office of this person, who is not even the governor of a small state? Did I not come on time, for fear of missing him? Is this the way Minos Zacharias, billionaire, acts? Could it be that Minos Zacharias is not really a billionaire? Maybe we should reconsider our loan? And tell our friends? Leverage works both ways, Mrs. Gold. It enables a relatively small sum of money to raise mountains. But if that small sum of money disappears, the mountains come crashing down again, very fast."

"But only those two assistants know. They've been with you for years, you said."

"As I was leaving, I noticed a tiny change in the attitude of the English girl. If someone else had seen it, someone as observant as myself—and investment bankers are *very* observant—it might have caused a small change in the attitude of the house I was dealing with, and that . . . For want of a nail, Mrs. Gold—"

"I can reverse the situation, Mr. Zacharias. Easily."

"Nothing is completely reversible, Mrs. Gold, as Heraclitus implied, but yes, it would help if Mr. Gold were to call me several times and hold on for a full ten minutes, request an appointment, and then wait in my anteroom for a full hour."

"In return for which . . . ?"

"Surely, Mrs. Gold, there is something that is more important to Mr. Gold than an hour of his time?"

"Many things, Mr. Zacharias, but can you provide one of them?"

"We shall see, Mrs. Gold. Now can we talk business?"

I'll give the guy credit; once he found out where the power was in that room, he didn't take his eyes off mine for one second, not even when Pearl, who had to have taken it as a personal insult, let her short little skirt creep up past the tops of her stockings.

"I would like to retain A.I.K., Inc., Private Investigators, to find the murderer of Thea Malabar, with Alexander Magnus Gold retained as consultant. There is a time limit of one week."

"What is your interest in finding the killer, Mr. Zacharias?"

"To see justice done, Mrs. Gold."

"With all due respect, Mr. Zacharias, bullshit. Cretan bullshit."

"Then accept this reason: Thea Malabar's murder was a personal insult to me. She was killed while I watched. And I could do nothing. Where I come from, came from, to have your lover killed in front of you, and to do nothing, is much worse than . . . than to be a passive, a contented cuckold. It is like to slap a father in front of his children. You not only cause the pain, you emphasize the helplessness of the one you hurt; you show that he cannot stop you from doing anything you want to him, anywhere, anytime. In my position, I cannot permit that."

"You also loved her, didn't you?"

"For many years. She was the only one I could . . . could feel as an equal. Her capacity for . . . for everything was equal to mine. There were times, had it been possible . . . I had considered marriage."

"Your wife stood in the way?"

"My wife never stood in my way; she helped me in every way possible. I do not undertake personal obligations lightly."

"But after her death—?"

"It was not a fitting time. And our paths, Thea's and mine, did not cross very often. Now that my year of mourning is over, I have been seeing—as you have no doubt researched these past three hours—Patricia Horgan. These personal questions—another example of the thoroughness of Alexander Magnus Gold Associates, also known as A.I.K., Inc.?"

"You seem to have researched *us* thoroughly, Mr. Zacharias."

"I had all night." He shrugged. "I assume you did the same." I waved at the thick pile of printouts on the desk. "Good," he said. "That will save some time."

"We charge high fees for Mr. Gold's services."

"But you collect only if you succeed. And you pay all the expenses."

"There have been some slight changes, now that we're licensed private investigators. In addition to the consultant's contingency fee, A.I.K. charges one thousand dollars per day or fraction thereof, plus out-of-office expenses." I hoped Pearl wouldn't giggle; this was the first time she had heard of our new fee schedule.

"You have never done that before." His face was flushed, angry.

"That's the way it is now," I said calmly.

"Are you deliberately charging me more than anyone else? Because I am Minos Zacharias?"

"There's the Yellow Pages, Mr. Z.," I said. "Help yourself. You get one free call for having wasted the trip."

He cooled rapidly, and smiled. "Just testing, Mrs. Gold."

"Testing costs, Mr. Z."

"There are limits, Mrs. Gold."

"When I thought Alexander was going to die, Mr. Z., I would have given anything for one more hour with him."

"I am not in that position, Mrs. Gold."

"So why are you here, Mr. Z.?" He was about to respond, but I put my hand out to stop. "We could go on like this all day," I said, "and I'd enjoy it tremendously. But you can't win. First, English is your second language, and second, I'm the fastest lip on the Upper West Side of New York, the put-down capital of the universe. So I'll do you a favor, Mr. Z. I'll declare myself the winner. Pearl and Burton will swear never to reveal to a soul your shameful secret: That you were bested at something by a woman and, as a consolation prize, Alexander and I will grovel in your office for free, *after* he finds the killer. Now can we talk business?"

He smiled ruefully. "I didn't realize . . . the competitive spirit . . . One gets carried away. Yes. I understand that you would consider a larger donation in your honor to a charity of your choice in lieu of a fee?"

"Not this time, Mr. Z. I want the fee to be paid directly to us; I'll let my accountant figure out how to save a little from the clutches of the I.R.S."

"I am willing to give your charity twice—"

"No."

"You seem very determined, Mrs. Gold, to make it very difficult for me to retain you."

"It took you long enough to figure it out."

"Why, Mrs. Gold? You never saw me before, I am sure of that. Have I, unknowingly, hurt someone close to you? In business, there can be widespread effects that no one—" I shook my head. "You are too intelligent to bring me here just to refuse me. So you intend to work with me, and I with you. If this is your way of raising the price, surely you must realize that even I have my limits." Though his words were calm, he looked as though he had difficulty holding in his anger.

"You really want to know, Mr. Z.?" He nodded, firmly. I stood up. "Then I invite you for lunch. I have a freezer full of goodies: American, Jewish, Greek." He raised an eyebrow. "I am a very good cook, Mr. Z. I have a lentil soup, peasant style, better than your mother used to make. You will stink of garlic all day, but you will kiss my hands after the third bowl." He smiled, really smiled, for the first time, I am sure, since he saw Thea Malabar killed in front of his eyes.

"Stay here," I said, "and make small talk, *only* small talk, with Alexander and Burton. Pearl and I will go upstairs. When the aroma becomes unendurable, come up."

"Done," he said, and leaned back in his easy chair. "And would you please order Mrs. Hanslik to change her skirt? I find it very distracting."

I know he said it just to make Pearl feel good.

14

"**A**re you crazy, Norma?" Pearl said. "Picking on him like that? Alex is ready to kill you."

"Don't worry," I said. "It's in the bag. He's hooked good. And don't change your skirt. You look terrific; even Burton was gaping." She looked surprised. After twenty-six years, husbands don't notice if you paint your nose purple. "It's true," I assured her. "Here's an apron. Make garlic croutons."

"That was, indeed, better than my mother used to make." Zacharias sipped his 120-proof slivovitz cautiously. "But she couldn't afford the ingredients you used. That was surely green Spanish virgin olive oil."

"I really enjoy cooking for people who understand food," I said, as Pearl removed the coffee cups. "You are hereby invited to the victory dinner after Alexander catches the killer."

"Ah, you are now ready to tell me why you are putting obstacles in the way of our working together."

"One, you didn't call like one human being who needs another."

"I explained that."

"You didn't apologize."

"An oversight; I am not accustomed to apologizing," he said. "I hereby apologize." It sounded sincere, but he didn't really look sorry.

"Then, the very rich are so much more powerful than ordinary people, the only time we have a chance of equalizing the odds is when they want something from us that they can't get by other means."

"I would hardly classify this company as 'ordinary people,' Mrs. Gold. But you're wrong about powerful people not being able to get things by other means. The Russians have proved that."

Having just refilled the brandy glasses, I was standing near Alexander, so I put my hands on his shoulders, full weight, hard. His muscles were very tight; I hoped it was from frustration at not being able to enter this discussion. "If my husband thought," I said, "that this was anything but rhetoric, you'd be dead right now." Burton looked tense too. "So pull in your claws, Mr. Z.; we know you have them."

"And you pull in yours, Mrs. Gold," he said coolly. "I knew you had claws too, before I came here. I have come to talk business, not to fight. Although I had made the decision before I came here, I am now certain that the man who has been married to you for twenty-eight years is the very man I need. Does that sound like the prelude to hard bargaining? Name your fee."

"You know how we work?"

"You wager that you can find the murderer within a limited time, and you pay all the expenses you incur." I must have moved, or something. "Yes, yes, Mrs. Gold, I have not forgotten the fee and expenses to A.I.K., although that was not expected. If you succeed, you get the entire fee. If you fail to produce the murderer within the alloted period, you get nothing."

"There's one more thing. We will use Burton Hanslik's firm for research, legal advice, and, uh, contacts with the police department. You pay for that too."

"I retain an excellent law firm. You may use them."

"No."

"They are very competent and respected, Mrs. Gold. Ask Mr. Hanslik."

I turned to Burton. He cleared his throat and spoke carefully. "They are respected for their legal skills."

"There, Mr. Z.," I said. "Not quite the highest compliment there is. Besides, they report to you."

"You would keep information from me?"

"You're entitled to the name of the killer, Mr. Z. That's it."

"The police must be satisfied too, Mrs. Gold."

"The police must arrest the killer for a crime arising out of the death of Thea Malabar."

"Just arrest? Crime *arising* out of the death? Not murder?"

"The way the laws in this town work, a guy who sets off a bomb in Bloomingdale's may be charged with littering the streets without a permit. Also, if the killer is insane, dead, or out of town, provided the police close their books on the case, we still collect."

"Agreed. What is the fee?"

"One million dollars." I looked at Alexander out of the corner of my eye. He stared straight ahead, his face absolutely blank. This was my play, so it was my decision. If I was wrong, I'd hear about it later; boy, would I hear about it. I had purposely kept it low—for a billionaire, that is—to ensure that Zacharias would not walk out; I knew how badly Alexander wanted a client.

Zacharias nodded. "I'll have my office mail you a retainer for A.I.K.'s expenses." He stood up.

"No retainer," I said. "Payment in full. In advance."

He raised his eyebrows. "Very well. I'll send A.I.K. a check for five thousand. What do you estimate for your services for the week, Mr. Hanslik?"

I nodded to Burton. "It's hard to say," he said. "For the Belmont case, which ran three days, the bill was almost fifteen thousand."

"For seven days, Mr. Z.," I said without blinking, "that's thirty-five thousand. And A.I.K. gets seven thousand for the week, not five; no rest for the wicked. Plus one thousand deposit for A.I.K.'s expenses. Total, forty-three thousand."

"And if Mr. Gold finds the killer in five days?" he asked sarcastically.

"We keep it all. Bonus for fast action." Minos Zacharias looked like he would be pawing the ground and charging in one minute. I didn't think it was the money, although it may have been—the wealthy are more careful with money than poor people—but the way I kept slipping the knife in, an inch at a time. He definitely did not like not being in full control of the situation. But the one advantage of the salami-slice technique is that when you're already in for twenty-seven slices, the twenty-eighth slice doesn't seem all that important.

"I'll send you a check for forty-three thousand dollars," he said brusquely. "Have Mr. Hanslik send the contract to my attorneys."

"Good," I said sweetly. "And as soon as the check clears and the contract is returned signed, we'll start working."

Minos Zacharias sat down fast. "The deadline is next Friday," he growled. "We have an agreement."

"The deadline is seven days from the time we have the money, Mr. Zacharias." I kept my voice soft. "A contract must include a transfer of values. You see any values transferred around here lately?"

He quieted down at once, looking only slightly upset. I'm

sure he regretted showing his true feelings. "It takes a week, at least, for a local check to clear," he said. "But if it makes you feel any better, I'll give you my personal check now." He reached into his breast pocket.

"Don't bother, Mr. Z.," I said. The moment of truth was upon us, and I'd be damned if I'd be the first to cry "hold enough." "I don't believe you'd waste interest by carrying forty-three thousand in a personal checking account. I know, I know"—I waved away his objection—"you'll transfer the money from one of your corporate accounts as soon as you get back to the office. Or use your overdraft. But it's past two o'clock on a Friday, so if you were to be so mean as to stop the check, we wouldn't know about it until the evil killer had been in jail for three days. That isn't exactly what I'd call paying in advance."

"I thought we had a good rapport, Mrs. Gold. Respect and even, on my side certainly, admiration. If that's how you feel about me, perhaps we should not do business together."

"Come off it, Mr. Z.," I said lightly. "I can't believe that billionaires let personal feelings interfere with business. I'm sure you've been called worse by some people you're working with right now. Feelings have nothing to do with it; it's the printouts. There are too many lawsuits in there for, shall we say, questions of interpretations of the contract after the party of the second part delivered the goods. You do have very skillful lawyers, as Burton said. I really don't think I should have to sue for my money, do you, Mr. Z.?"

He glared at me sullenly. "What would you have me do, Mrs. Gold?"

"You're stalling, Mr. Z. Even Pearl knows that you can phone the president of your bank and transfer forty-three thousand dollars to A.I.K.'s account in one minute, and record the transaction here on our computer. Tell him you'll be by later to sign the papers; he'll wait for an important client like you. Here's our account and branch number; coincidently, we use the same bank." What I didn't tell him was that, as soon as we got word that the transfer had been completed, I'd have my banker electronically transfer A.I.K.'s entire account to Burton's, in a bank that Zacharias did not use. Or control.

He gave it one last try. "How can I pay you without a contract? This is unbusinesslike."

"Burton has a contract all ready," I said. "All that's needed is to fill in the blanks. In ink. Takes two minutes." I held out my hand. Burton gave me two copies of the contract we'd used for Max Baron, modified as I had required. I handed them to Zacharias. "Sign here," I said.

"I don't sign anything without my lawyers," he said.

"Sure. Take your time. No rush. And after they make changes, Burton will want to make changes. And so on. Figure three months. Minimum."

He looked at me and decided I wasn't kidding. He was also sure, I could read it in his look, that I was not thinking about the ace up his sleeve. So sure, and maybe also to clinch the misdirection, that he signed one copy without reading it, pushed it over to me, and went to the phone and ordered the transfer of funds.

When he came back, the contracts were still in front of me, unsigned. When he saw that, one muscle in his jaw twitched, that's all—he had amazing control—but he said nothing, though he must have known what was coming.

"I deliberately didn't sign the contract, Mr. Z.," I said, "to give you a chance to back out. If you decide to do that, we'll tear your signature off the contract and I'll get on the phone with you and cancel the transfer of funds."

"Why would I want to do that, Mrs. Gold?" He was playing

dumb; not going to go down without a fight. A fight he wanted? On his head be it.

"We haven't arranged how you are going to pay the million dollars, Alexander's fee, in advance."

"I did not agree to pay that in advance," he said. "That was only to be paid when earned. If earned." The fish was still flopping.

"And I did not agree that I'd have to sue you to get the money after it was earned. And certainly, not in a Greek court, since it would be easy for you to be out of the U.S. for a year or two. Or forever." The misericord, right between the forth and fifth ribs. "Burton will tell you how it will be done."

Burton kept his voice dry and lawyerly. "You will deposit the million dollars in an escrow account maintained by me. I will release it to A.I.K. upon the fulfillment of the conditions noted in the contract on or before two P.M., Eastern Standard Time, Friday, or to you, Mr. Zacharias, if the conditions are not fulfilled by that time. Here is the bank information and the account number. All is arranged; the transfer can be made by phone."

"I can manage forty-three thousand." Zacharias' voice was calm, relaxed. He had lost, but really nothing was lost. He had not been tricked, or swindled, or fooled. All that had happened was that, if what Zacharias had contracted for was done, he would pay what he had agreed to pay, rather than cheat the man who had performed the job. Also, he had been acting as if it was a foregone conclusion that Alexander would solve the case within a week; after all, hadn't he solved three other impossible cases? On the other hand, what if Alexander couldn't do it? We'd be out a lot of money, especially if Alexander decided to reenact the crime, the way he did with the Boguslav murder. Opera performances have to cost more than ballets; and I'd hate to tell you what that ballet caper cost us.

"I explained before"—Zacharias hadn't bothered to even look at the paper Burton had put before him—"that I am not like your friend Belmont, or even Max Baron. They have real property; I deal in ephemeral things. I need my cash, or the appearance of cash, all the time, and I use it with great leverage. To remove a million in cash from my control would be disastrous." He paused. "I'll give you a note, to hold in escrow."

"The name of the escrow account," Burton said, "is Minos Zacharias Reserve Account No. 73. It will appear to everyone, even your banker, that you still control that account. And that there are a great many more like it scattered around the world. And it's only for a week."

Zacharias was licked, and he knew it. He quietly went to the phone and did what he had to do. Then he turned back and addressed me. "Mrs. Gold—Norma, if I may—this has been a most interesting afternoon. I wish I had met you thirty years ago. In Crete. Thank you for a truly excellent lunch. Thank you, Mr. Hanslik, for I am sure you had a good deal to do with the, er, smoothness of this transaction. It may be that we will do business together, on the same side of the table, I hope, in the future. Thank you, Mrs. Hanslik. I hope we can meet again, when you are not in costume and not under orders not to talk. And, Mr. Gold, I regret you were, er, unable to talk with me; I was looking forward to meeting you properly. Now, if there are no more surprises, good day to you all." He started for the door.

"One more surprise," Alexander growled. " I'm not going to do it."

15

One of these days, and today would be the perfect day to do it, I am going to cut Alexander into seventeen equal pieces with a rusty knife. Not that I have a fetish for prime numbers, but because it's impossible to cut a human body, or even my husband's body, into seventeen equal pieces quickly and easily. Four is like nothing; once down, once across, presto, four equal pieces. Six is almost as fast. So is eight, if you put one piece on top of the other and use a machete. But a prime number of equal chunks has to be done by trial and error. Hack off a lump, weigh it, cut off a bit, add a snippet; it could take days. Weeks, if you put your mind to it. The Death of a Thousand Cuts. Two thousand, if I worked it carefully. And he deserved it. If anyone deserved to suffer, it was Alexander Magnus Gold, The Undependable. Or The Dependable, depending how you looked at it.

On him, I could always count. To screw things up, I mean. Here, today, based only on hearsay and the information in the printouts, I had conceived a wonderful plan. Planned a terrific conception. In only three hours. Implemented an unbelievable deal in which I brought one of the shrewdest, slickest, unscrupulousest, most famous jet-set billionaires in the world to his knees, practically. Had him even proposing marriage, sort of. Retroactively. And it wasn't just my lentil soup either. He even didn't almost notice Pearl in a low-cut, with her skirt all the way up to her *pupick*. And Alexander decided, just plain decided, to throw it all away.

For what? Well may you ask. For jealousy, that's for what. Just plain jealousy. He couldn't *bear* that I should do something brilliant. Not only brilliant, but workable, practical, concrete. *He* had to be the big genius of the family. Would it have killed him to admit that I was smarter than him? Or even made him a little bit sick? And not even smarter; how about *just* as smart? Or even in the same league? No. He had to ruin my triumph, just as Minos Zacharias, beaten but gracious, was ready to leave the battlefield, not quite on his shield, but not with banners bravely flying either. And I wouldn't have told anyone—not that it's such a crime that the wife has a brain too—*I* wouldn't have made it public. Pearl I could depend on for that. Alexander always forgives her, so no harm done. But next time, and I really mean it this time, next time he gets into trouble, I'm going to let him sweat until he begs, actually *begs,* for me to save his fat neck. Which I may or may not do, depending on how nice he's been lately.

"We have a contract, Mr. Gold," Zacharias said. "Drawn by your own attorney. The money has been transferred. There has been a meeting of the minds."

"Oh, I'll fulfill the terms of the contract," Alexander said. "All I meant was that I know I can't find the killer."

"Giving up before you start, Mr. Gold? This is not like what I've heard of you."

"It's all your fault, Mr. Zacharias." Zacharias looked puzzled. "Groucho Marx," Alexander said.

"I fail to see—"

"I don't remember the name of the movie," Alexander continued. "I lost brain cells when I had the heart attack, but Groucho and Chico were working out a contract, tearing it to pieces, literally, until there was no contract left at all. The point was that the contract was not intended to be a real agreement, it was just a device to allow some gags to be played out."

Zacharias' face was red; Alexander must have touched a deep nerve. "I signed that contract in good faith, and Mrs. Gold signed it too. If this is an attempt to increase the price, I warn you there is a limit to my patience."

"Not at all, Mr. Zacharias. As far as I am concerned, you can take your forty-three thousand dollars back right now. Under the present conditions, I cannot find the killer."

Zacharias turned back from the door and sat down in his chair again. "I find it very—very *interesting* to deal with the Golds. Tell me, sir, why you cannot give me what I am paying you for?"

"Oh, I can give you that," Alexander said. "I just can't find the murderer with you opposing me."

Zacharias tapped the arm of his chair with his fingers; he must have been deeply upset. "I have agreed to pay you one million dollars to find the killer of Thea Malabar. To me that does not sound like opposing you."

At this, Alexander leaned back against his big black chair with an air of certainty, of knowing he was right. "Mr. Zacharias, you heard every word I said, and understood it. That you chose to respond only to the last part of my statement . . . You are not *paying* me anything to find the murderer; you are *betting* me a million that I do *not* find him. You are *paying* A.I.K. forty-three thousand, much against your will, to have me *look* as though I'm looking for the killer for a week, and you will do everything you can to avoid losing your million-dollar bet."

"Why are you going through this ridiculous . . . ? I am a busy man, Mr. Gold."

"I apologize for wasting your time," Alexander said. "Burton, please void the contract and return the money and escrow to Mr. Zacharias at once. Norma will show you to the door, sir. Good day."

Minos Zacharias did not move. He was taking slow deep breaths, the kind Alexander has to take when he gets overly upset, to slow his pulse. Alexander, I saw, was breathing normally.

After two full minutes, Alexander spoke, quietly. "Granted, Mr. Zacharias, that I am the best for this kind of case. But there are other very good investigators in New York. These agencies cost much less than six thousand dollars a day. Why not retain one of them?" Zacharias did not answer. Alexander went on, still quietly, "My wife gave you a very bad time, insulted you, in fact, if you will replay the discussion in your mind. Billionaires do not have to stand for insult, or even annoyance. You did. Why? You had no qualms about a million-dollar contingency fee, but almost choked at a forty-three-thousand-dollar firm payment. Why? When my wife stymied all your attempts to avoid payment of the fee, you agreed to all of her conditions, including the escrow of a million dollars, although you knew none of our other clients had done this before. Why? Put it all together, Mr. Zacharias, what does this show?"

"You tell me, Mr. Gold," Zacharias said nastily. "And when you are done, I may very well accept your offer to tear up the contract."

"You came here on a business matter involving a million dollars without your attorneys. Without even your secretary. Is that the way you usually work, Mr. Zacharias?"

"Mrs. Gold seemed to enjoy waving the red flag at me. I

could not afford any more of this foolishness in front of my associates."

"It is clear, Mr. Zacharias, that you had to have Alexander Magnus Gold under any conditions, at any cost. Why? You don't know me. I've been in business, this business, only a few months, and I've had only three murder cases. What do these cases have in common? The victims were in the arts, were very important people, internationally known, and the fees, though extraordinarily high, were contingency fees. No solution, no pay. Further, the murders were, essentially, impossible crimes. If you wanted to persuade someone that you had retained the best possible man for the job, to impress him that you were really, seriously, trying to find the killer of Thea Malabar, you had to use me."

"There is no one to impress, Mr. Gold. I was really trying to get the best possible man for the job."

"Another advantage for you, Mr. Zacharias, was that I would cost you nothing. Everyone, at least in your circles, knows that I work on a contingency basis."

"May I point out, Mr. Gold, that I did not walk out when you cost me forty-three thousand dollars for a week's work and I was forced to tie up a million for the week as well."

"May I suggest, Mr. Zacharias, that you had no choice. I am sure that, if my wife had the courage"—now it comes out; it was really all *my* fault—"to double all the numbers, you would still not have walked out. You could have gotten the second-best man in New York for a thousand a week and a ten thousand bonus. Why didn't you, Mr. Zacharias? What could be worth as much to you as you are paying me?"

"You can't change the deal, Mr. Gold. We have a contract."

"You haven't checked me out well enough, Mr. Zacharias; I would honor my wife's word even if *I* had to pay *you*. But again, you're evading my question. The answer is, obviously, it is your life that is worth that much to you."

"As it is to any man, Mr. Gold. But there is no connection."

"And why the one-week limit?" Alexander pressed on. "What's the deadline?"

"I do not enjoy keeping a million dollars tied up for even one week, Mr. Gold."

"You must be under even more tension than I had imagined, Mr. Zacharias, to have made that slip. You set the one-week limit long before Norma mentioned escrowing the money." Zacharias glared openly at Alexander. I decided, in the future, to carry my little gun at all times, even in the house. "Since there is nothing in the crime that I'm aware of, or in the schedule of the Pantheon Opera Company, to make any deadline necessary, the reason must be inherent in your operations."

"That is my business, Mr. Gold." Zacharias stood up. "I have a signed contract. I have transferred the money. If you do not perform as contracted, I will sue you. As Mr. Hanslik said, my lawyers are very skilled. You will be a pauper."

"Please don't insult my intelligence, Mr. Zacharias." Alexander was calm. "First of all, you have no contract with me; you have a contract with A.I.K. Second, A.I.K. is a corporation; if you win, you may take all their assets, which, if sold at auction, might pay for one hour of your attorneys' fees. Third, if my wife and Mrs. Hanslik decide to fight your suit, I have no doubt Burton Hanslik will represent them. He too is a highly skilled attorney."

"I am not blackmailed easily, Mr. Gold," Zacharias said, "as you have no doubt found in your researches." He waved at the pile of printouts.

"If you mean the paternity suits?" Alexander said. "Ten years ago? Yes, I read about them. Three at once."

"I led them on, Mr. Gold, until in court I provided medical evidence of my unfortunate bout with mumps. They had invested huge sums of borrowed money setting this trap for me, money they were unable to repay, assuming that I would settle out of court for the nuisance value, at least."

"Then you filed blackmail charges against them, Zacharias, and made sure they went to jail. You went to a lot of trouble you could easily and cheaply have avoided."

"True, but I was never troubled by blackmailers again, Gold. Keep that in mind."

"This skirmishing is really unnecessary," Alexander said. "It is now obvious that my reasoning is correct. Therefore, if you wish, I will give you, right now, a handwritten letter stating that I refuse to consult for you, explaining why I refuse, and that I will personally take full responsibility for the breach of contract, so that you can make me a pauper. Is that what you want, Zacharias?"

I was ready to kill Alexander. Again he was making the grand gesture, betting his life, our lives, on what had to be a very shaky chain of logic based on an even wobblier set of assumptions. What that chain of logic was, what the assumptions were, was, naturally, beyond me. But suddenly Minos Zacharias folded. Collapsed. He aged ten years, right as I watched. "What do you want, Gold?" he whispered.

"An intelligent decision, Mr. Zacharias." Alexander was suspiciously gracious. "But you really had no alternative, did you? The deadline could only be that you were going back to Crete, the center of your operations, in a week. For whatever reason, you absolutely must go back there, and it will be a very long stay, certainly months. Maybe forever. Right, Mr. Zacharias?"

"It has become necessary for me to be in Crete for an extended period of time, Mr. Gold. Business."

"So what would happen, Mr. Zacharias, when you went back to Crete? What were you afraid of? You said it before; your life is worth a million to you. Or everything you've got, if you come right down to it."

"I have enemies all over the world, Mr. Gold. They may hate me, but none of them has ever tried to kill me. And certainly, there is no one *you* could protect me from; you're not a body-guard."

"I can protect you from the one man you clearly fear, if that man really believes you are *truly* trying to find the murderer of Thea Malabar."

"Isn't it clear that is exactly what I am doing, Gold?"

"What is clear to me, Zacharias, is that you want to give the appearance of trying to find the murderer, but don't really want him found."

"You seem certain of my guilt, Gold. When you check further, you will find I am innocent."

"I don't know if you killed Thea Malabar or not," Alexander said, "or your wife. The point I am making is that it would not have been very hard to convince the actual killer that the guy who hired him was an emissary of Minos Zacharias. How hard, in fact, would it have been to convince the *emissary* that the guy hiring him came directly from Zacharias? No, Zacharias, innocent or guilty, you cannot afford to have the killer found."

"You think I did not figure this out myself, Gold?" Zacharias said wearily. "I know I did not kill Thea, or my wife either, or order them killed, as many people think, but if I cannot persuade you, my own detective, that I did not, how can I persuade others?"

"You had the power and you had the motive, Zacharias."

"I had no motive," he said, his face strained. "I loved Helen. I really loved my wife. She understood what I did, what I had to do, and why I did it. She supported me in everything. I would never have left her, she knew that, so why would I kill her?"

"I will discover that in time, Zacharias."

"What is it you want, Gold? What do you really want?"

"Why, to find the killer, Mr. Zacharias. What else?"

"If I do not stop you—"

"No one can stop me," Alexander said, very softly.

"I will not *hinder* you, Gold, I promise. And if you, somehow, find out who the killer is, in return you must tell me first."

"So you can have him killed, Zacharias, before he talks?"

"I cannot afford to . . . to be framed for this murder, Gold."

"I will find the truth, Zacharias, the whole truth. If you are innocent, you have nothing to fear."

"No one is wholly innocent, Gold. But I had nothing to do with the murder of Thea Malabar."

"And the murder of Helen Taramakis Zacharias? The murder of your wife?"

"There is no way to prove my innocence, Gold. Not in seven days, not in seven years."

"I don't want an unwilling client, Zacharias, and especially not a hostile, dangerous client, one who may be a murderer," Alexander mused. "But if I find the murderer of your wife, and it is not you, that will prove your innocence."

"Criminals can be bribed to say anything, Gold. I did not retain you to look for the murderer of my wife. I do not want you to assume, even, that she was murdered. She was not. You must concentrate only on Thea Malabar."

"And if the two cases are connected?"

"They are not connected, Gold. Positively not. You will make a million dollars if you find the killer of Thea Malabar, Gold; do you want to give that up? You have seven days, Gold, seven days to solve an impossible crime. How can you do it, how can you *begin* to do it, if you are thinking of a . . . a disappearance of a year ago, of five thousand miles away? Don't be a fool, Gold. Take the million, if you can."

"You cannot stop me from thinking, Zacharias. Even I cannot stop that."

"Think all you want, Gold, but remember, I paid you to look

into the Malabar murder. Nothing else. You took my money, Gold, to do a specific job. You owe me your full attention for seven days; your full concentration."

"You pose an interesting puzzle, Zacharias," Alexander said. "Even if I wanted to, I cannot drop the case now. Too many people know you came here, including Max Baron. If I dropped the case now, for whatever reason, Helen's father, the super-rich Demo Taramakis, would have you tortured and killed, and I'm not sure you deserve that, at least for these two murders. But you cannot have me killed either. Taramakis would have you flayed if I died now, even of apparently natural causes. If you harm, or even threaten to harm, my wife"—here Alexander's voice grew very soft—"you will *beg* me to turn you over to Taramakis. And regardless of what you promise, if I even *think* you are trying to hinder me, I will announce my suspicions to the papers. How would you resolve this little dilemma, Zacharias?"

Minos Zacharias thought for a moment. "I will retain you, for the fee already paid, within the same seven-day period, to find the murderer of my wife, *if* she was murdered. If you find proof that I was the killer, or ordered the killing, you must tell me twenty-four hours before you tell anyone else."

"If you killed your wife, Zacharias, I wouldn't give you that chance to escape punishment. No, I don't want you to retain me to look into the murder of Helen Taramakis Zacharias, unless the two murders are connected, and I don't know if they are, yet. If I fail, you could use my lack of success as evidence of your innocence in one or even both murders. And I am not sure you are innocent. Of either."

"Then what do you want, Gold?" Zacharias sounded tired.

"It is clear to me, Zacharias, that whatever you promise, you will do your best to keep me from finding the murderer of Thea Malabar. I need someone who will *want* me to find the killer, who will actively help me. I need someone who can *make* the suspects cooperate with me."

"You have a plan, Gold? What do you *really* want?"

"Sign an addendum to the contract," Alexander said, "authorizing A.I.K. to accept another client, a joint client, who will also retain us to find the killer of Thea Malabar. I will announce the name of the murderer to both of you at the same time."

Zacharias thought for a moment. "Very well. But his commission must coincide with mine; that is, to search for the killer of Thea Malabar."

"Are you sure that there is no connection between the murder of Thea Malabar and the disappearance of your wife?"

"I assure you there is none."

"I cannot help wondering, Mr. Zacharias, how you would know that with such certainty."

"I don't care what you wonder, Mr. Gold; I know in my heart that there can be no connection. My brief to you is to find the killer of Thea Malabar, in the allotted time. You are also permitted to retain an additional client for *exactly* the same function." He turned to Burton. "Add that by hand, Hanslik; we will all sign now. I want Mr. Gold's personal signature on this too, in return for permitting the additional client to ride on my coattails."

Burton was writing as Zacharias spoke. Alexander signed without reading, then Zacharias signed and turned to leave. "I have spent more time here than I intended," he said. "Now I must go. I wish you both"—he looked directly at me—"many long years together."

For all I know, it could have been sincere, but to me, it sounded like a Chinese curse. Especially if it was sincere.

16

"Why you, Alexander?" I asked as soon as the door closed on Zacharias. "I know you're a genius and all that, but why did he pick you? Or anyone else, for that matter?"

"Who would kill Zacharias when he got back to Crete?" Alexander asked in reply. "And why?"

"Demetrios Taramakis?" Pearl said, hesitantly.

"Of course," Alexander said. "Zacharias' father-in-law. Helen's father."

"But he wasn't on the yacht when . . . when she disappeared," Pearl said.

"Try to think like an old man, Pearl, the way an old-fashioned man thinks," Alexander said. "An old man who is one of the richest men in Greece. Helen, his only child, is married to Minos Zacharias, a man he never liked. Zacharias, who does not deal in honest products, tangibles such as olives, oil, ships; who deals, rather, in intangibles, in speculation and arbitrage, a man who is not even a real Greek—"

"Crete is part of Greece," Pearl pointed out.

"Some Cretans don't think so," Alexander said. "Else why is he named Minos?" He pointed to the printouts about Zacharias.

"The Minoan culture is much older than the Greek, and lasted for two thousand years. That Zacharias is a Greek citizen by birth is irrelevant to Taramakis; in his eyes, Zacharias is a barbarian. That barbarian, the man his only child married, this Cretan, in Taramakis' mind, used Helen's dowry and his father-in-law's name to build up his own fortune. This man had love affairs all through the marriage, openly. This man kept his long-time mistress, Thea Malabar, near him much of the time, sometimes even escorting her and his wife to the same event. This man never denied Malabar's statement that she and Zacharias were planning to marry. If you were Demo Taramakis, how would you feel?"

"Zacharias said that his wife supported him in everything," Pearl, the trusting, said. "There might have been a business reason for everything he did."

Alexander ignored this. "Then, one night, in the middle of the Mediterranean, Helen Taramakis Zacharias disappears. Overboard? Of course. But who did it? Was Thea Malabar tired of waiting? Did Minos Zacharias promise to marry Thea as soon as his wife was out of the way?"

"The inquiry exonerated Zacharias completely," Pearl said. "I researched it. The yacht turned back within one-half hour after Helen was last seen. The captain spent all night searching the area, but only her scarf was found. Helen was a strong swimmer. If she fell, or was pushed, she could have stayed afloat for hours. The only conclusion possible was suicide."

"Why should she kill herself, Pearl?"

"Who knows what is in the heart of another, Alex?"

"Even your own wife? Zacharias surely would have mentioned something in his defense if Helen ever gave him the slightest reason to suspect suicide."

"Even a wife, yes. *Especially* a wife. Ask Norma, someday." This was very daring of Pearl; she had never said anything like this, even close to this, before. I knew she was addressing Burton, trying to get a message across to Burton, but I wish she hadn't involved me. I wondered what I would say if Alexander ever asked me. Nothing, of course, if I wanted to stay married to him, and I did, very much. But he would never ask. He thinks life with him has to be a bowl of cherries, and if it isn't always perfectly perfect, then all I have to do is practice a little harder.

"Maybe it was a case of mistaken identity?" Alexander mused. "Someone who wanted Thea Malabar out of the way? A first murder attempt that failed? A sailor would have no qualms about throwing Thea Malabar overboard if his boss suggested it."

"That may be," Pearl said, "but if it was, it wasn't mistaken identity. Helen was much taller than Thea, much bigger all over. No one could mistake one for the other."

"Salome Auber, then?"

"She has short blond hair," Pearl said, "and Helen had long black hair. And again, Helen Zacharias was taller, broader, athletically built."

"All right, so it couldn't have been mistaken identity. And while it might have been, possibly, suicide, I don't believe it and I don't believe Demetrios Taramakis believes it. And what will Taramakis make of the fact that this cast of *Rigoletto* was on the yacht at the time Helen disappeared?"

"According to the papers," Pearl said, "and it made a big splash in Nice, the whole thing was Hugo Kreuz's idea. He arranged it with Helen Zacharias, in order to make the whole production harmonious. But Ettore D'Aquilla wasn't there; Thea wouldn't let him within a mile of her in a restricted place like a yacht, and she wouldn't go within a hundred miles of Sicily."

"It's also possible," I said, "that Minos Zacharias didn't

know about it in advance, either. Helen was the culture vulture; the only interest Minos had in opera was Thea Malabar."

"And Gregor Brezhnikov was only selected a few weeks ago," Pearl said, "so he wasn't there. And Hugo Kreuz doesn't even go out in a rowboat."

"Still," Alexander said, "there was the director and three of the five stars of this production of *Rigoletto* on board the yacht the night Helen Taramakis Zacharias disappeared. Can Demo Taramakis *not* make a connection between the two murders?"

"But Zacharias was not on the yacht at that time," Pearl said.

"Doubly suspicious to Taramakis," Alexander said. "Zacharias' business appointment couldn't wait until they docked in Candia two days later? This must have been the most damning fact of all to Taramakis, that he was *not* there. How easy it would have been for someone, at Zacharias' urging or bribing, to push Helen overboard."

"And now he has to go back to Greece?" I said. "To stay for a long time? Maybe forever, you said? That's why he was so anxious to pay by check, so our services would have cost him nothing when he canceled the checks. Fortunately for A.I.K., and you, Alexander, I stymied that."

"But what about his marriage to Patricia Horgan?" Pearl asked. "Doesn't he have to be in New York for that?"

"What could be more romantic than a wedding aboard his yacht, *La Belle Hélène?*" Alexander said, waving at the stack of printouts. "The yacht, incidentally, was his father-in-law's wedding present to Helen. A perfect gift, since she loved all water sports."

"Then why was there a deadline?" Pearl asked. "He doesn't have to be here for us to solve the case."

"The point is," Alexander said, "he isn't in the least bit interested in *solving* the case. Remember what he said about *appearing* to be rich at a time when he was really broke?

Zacharias wanted to appear to be doing everything possible to find the murderer of Thea Malabar, but he didn't want him found. Why?"

"He's the killer himself?" Pearl asked. "But he can't be. He was in the box next to the Barons' all the time. I saw him."

"Why didn't you point him out to me?" I asked.

"Everybody in the boxes was famous," Pearl said. "I thought you knew them all from their pictures."

"Can we please get back to the case?" Alexander sounded annoyed. What he really meant was, Would we please pay attention to his brilliant deductions. "Obviously Zacharias wasn't the killer of Thea Malabar, although he may have ordered the murder."

"But I thought he really loved Thea Malabar," I said. "Why didn't he marry her?"

"She was already married," Pearl said, "and divorce is unheard of in D'Aquilla's milieu."

"Are you saying," I asked, "that the *only* way for Malabar and Zacharias to marry was if his wife and her husband died?"

"It's obvious," Alexander said. "And Phase One had already been completed."

"Malabar kills Helen Zacharias and Zacharias kills Ettore D'Aquilla? Was that the deal?"

"I don't think so," Alexander said. "I don't see Zacharias as all that anxious to marry Malabar. It's the other way around; she wants to marry him. I'm sure he loved her, but I think he was perfectly satisfied to have her as his mistress. I don't believe he would take the risk of killing her husband, or having him killed, or anyone killed for that matter, unless his own life was at stake."

"But you said he might have ordered Malabar killed."

"His life was at stake there. She must have threatened to tell that Zacharias ordered her to kill his wife."

"He *ordered* Malabar? No one orders Malabar, and no court would believe that."

"Demetrios Taramakis would. He's the one man Zacharias fears. So it's perfectly logical to keep him on the list of suspects."

"But it isn't necessary to kill Malabar's husband," I said. "Couldn't she get an annulment from D'Aquilla?"

"After fifteen years? For an American politician, maybe, but for a Sicilian? Never. Romantic love, Norma, is a very recent invention, and even today, at certain levels, certain people cannot marry as they wish. They have to marry for reasons of state, to cement alliances, for survival, even."

"That's why he's marrying Patricia Horgan?"

"Obviously," Alexander interrupted us. "Now can we drop the gossip and get back to the case?" He waited a moment, as if daring Pearl and me to say something, then went on. "Taramakis was almost certain, before, that Zacharias induced Thea Malabar to push Helen overboard by promising to marry Thea. Now that Malabar has been murdered, he is absolutely certain. Taramakis tied up his daughter's estate in the Greek courts— he's very powerful in Athens—and Zacharias has had some serious business reverses this past year, assisted, no doubt, by Taramakis, which is why Zacharias had to hire me."

"I'm dizzy," Pearl said, truthfully I'm sure. "Why does that follow?"

"To Taramakis, obviously, Zacharias had Malabar killed so she could not confess he made her kill Helen. Zacharias left Europe two days after his wife died; he's been in the U.S. ever since. Only his lawyers appeared at the inquiry. Taramakis clearly has been spending a lot of time and money to force Zacharias to come back to Greece. Much as he tried to avoid it, Zacharias' affairs are now in such bad shape that he *must* go back, next week, at the latest. And in order to recoup his fortunes, he had to marry Patricia Horgan instead of Thea Malabar, so he had a double reason to get rid of Thea."

"But Patricia Horgan doesn't have much money," Pearl said. "How does marrying her—?"

"Appearance, as Zacharias himself described. She's world-famous, the granddaughter of a president, the niece of a governor, and she's in the papers every month. With her as his wife, Zacharias will have entrée to social and financial circles which were previously closed to him."

"And Thea Malabar"—I was beginning to get the picture—"found out about Patricia Horgan and threatened to tell Taramakis, unless Zacharias married *her,* that Minos swore he would marry her if only Helen fell overboard while he was gone. Accidentally. So Thea had to be killed before she talked. Now Taramakis is absolutely sure Zacharias arranged Helen's murder."

"That's a little hard to prove," Burton said. "It's an awful lot of guesswork."

"My *guesswork* fits all the known facts," Alexander said. "But it doesn't matter what you think, Burt; what matters is what Demetrios Taramakis believes. That's why Zacharias came here. He needed someone cheap, and he thought I'd be cheap, or at least that he could get away without paying me. I'm also sure he didn't believe I could find the killer—and that might be an interesting area to explore—so he was doubly safe. Safe financially and safe from punishment. What he needed to save his life was to show Demetrios Taramakis that he had hired the best; offered a million dollars—*that* Taramakis could understand—to someone who had solved three other impossible cases in similar circumstances. And most important, someone two other billionaires had used and trusted. Nothing persuades a billionaire so well of the value of anything or anyone as the imprimatur of other billionaires, and I'm the only one in the world

who has that. That's why he stood for Norma's insults and out-
rageous conditions. That's why he could not walk out when I
turned him down. All Taramakis had to hear was that I had
refused the case, that Zacharias had *let* me refuse the case, and
he would be doubly convinced that Zacharias did not want the
murderer of Thea Malabar found. In case the murderer might
talk, I mean."

"But couldn't Taramakis have Zacharias killed in New
York?" Burton asked. "Why go through all this to get him back
to Greece?"

"He probably could have," I answered that one. "Although it
would be much harder. And up till now, he wasn't a hundred
percent sure Zacharias was guilty. It's clear Taramakis planned
to string Zacharias up by his tongue and have a long, slow talk
with him, the discussion to last for weeks or as long as
Zacharias could have held out, while he decided how to *really*
hurt poor Minos, maybe even bringing in a few friends to show
what happens to anyone foolish enough to kill the daughter of a
billionaire. The long, slow chipping away of Zacharias' fortune—or credit, same thing in his world—was obviously part of
the plan. Phase One, the buildup, to give Zacharias time to
meditate on his sins."

"Exactly, Norma," Alexander said. "Which is why I was sure
that Zacharias would do anything to keep me from withdrawing
from the case, especially when I offered to write a letter explaining why I was refusing to consult for him. And that's what
I meant when I said I could give him what he was paying for—
the *appearance* of trying to find the murderer—but that I was
unable to find the killer with him opposing me."

"Do you really think Zacharias did it?" Pearl asked.

"Right now, it looks bad for him, but I have to find out a lot
more before I figure it out."

Sure. Find out how much we *don't* know. In books, the detective is always finding out more. In real life, *normal* real life, the detective learns *something*—no matter how little, it's something—from everybody he talks to. By us, the more we do, the more people tell us, the more we learn how little we know. Maybe what I should do is lock the doors, tear out the telephone, and take a week's worth of sleeping pills. Then, by next Friday, our deadline, I wouldn't know any less than I did the week before. Which would be a big improvement on what we have now.

17

"**M**r. Kreuz," Burton said, "you, or rather, the Pantheon Opera Company, owes Tay-Sachs a lot of money."

Hugo Kreuz, the general manager of the Pantheon Opera, was not wearing the usual Eric von Stroheim sneer I had seen in a hundred newspaper photos. His shaven head was shiny with sweat and his collar was limp. "The entire opera was performed," he said in his heavy accent, "except for a bit at the end."

"The contract you signed," Burton said, "does not mention 'excepts.' If even one of the principals did not give a complete performance, fifty percent of the fee must be refunded. The newspaper headlines are accusing you and the Pantheon of stupidity and incompetence for letting the world's greatest singer be murdered."

"The audience was completely satisfied, Mr. Hanslik." Kreuz said. "It was the greatest performance of *Rigoletto*, the greatest cast, of all time."

"We paid an extra hundred thousand to get that cast, Kreuz, so don't bring that up." Burton was firm. "The contract is clear; it does not mention audience satisfaction. But now that you bring it up, I can assure you the audience was *not* completely satisfied. I, Mrs. Hanslik, and my guests here, Mr. and Mrs. Gold, were very upset. Mr. Gold almost suffered another heart attack and Mrs. Gold suffered great anguish therefrom. Mr. and Mrs. Baron were most troubled as, I am sure, was most of the distinguished audience. In fact, I may just send a questionnaire to the list of ticket holders inquiring about how they were damaged by this horrible deed." Burton was really hamming it up; today, in Kreuz's office, he was playing the hardhearted villain. And loving it.

"You are trying to make a lawsuit, Hanslik," Kreuz was trying to contain his anger. "This is blackmail."

"In front of witnesses, Kreuz?" Burton smiled evilly. "Impugning the reputation of New York's leading attorney?"

"I have trouble with English; what I meant—"

"Your English, except for the accent, is perfect, Kreuz. I hope the Pantheon carries heavy insurance."

"Sickness, acts of God, accidents, yes." Kreuz actually took out his handkerchief and mopped his face. "Murder, I am not so sure; the attorneys are checking."

"This was willful negligence, Kreuz; I doubt that your insurance covers that."

"We have good security, Hanslik. How could anyone protect against killing on stage? In front of everybody. It is not possible. Look"—Kreuz smiled, sort of—"maybe we could work something out. On the Tay-Sachs money, I mean; the audience nonsense is out of the question."

"The Tay-Sachs refund is not open for discussion, Kreuz; the contract speaks for itself. And even if *we* don't bring suit on behalf of the audience, do you think I was the only attorney in the audience?"

"When I find who did it"—Kreuz lost control for a moment—"I will . . . I will . . ." His powerful hands opened and closed like claws.

"That's a great idea," Burton said, "but don't do it in front of witnesses. Unless, of course, you want more headlines."

"Do what?" Kreuz had regained his composure. "I was merely stretching my fingers. I intend to sue whoever did it, that is all."

"How will you find the murderer?"

"Captain Morgan, our chief of security, is looking into it. The police too. Lieutenant Warshafsky impressed me as being very efficient."

"A case like this"—Burton probed cautiously—"is so unusual that it's unlikely that Captain Morgan, or the police—"

"We also have movies, Hanslik, the TV movies that young Jeffrey Baron arranged. They will show who the murderer is."

"They haven't and they won't," Burton said. "Come on, Kreuz, it's Friday afternoon, almost twenty-four hours. If you could see the murderer in those movies, Warshafsky would have had him in custody by now. No one in the audience saw him and the movies don't show him either."

Kreuz leaned back in his chair, his face completely relaxed. This, evidently, was something he could handle. "You are going to make a suggestion, perhaps, Mr. Hanslik? A course of action you recommend?"

"Lieutenant Warshafsky, you can check with him, has found that Mr. Gold has been of great assistance in other difficult cases. Perhaps you can persuade him—?"

"I doubt that much persuasion will be necessary," Kreuz said drily, "especially since Mrs. Julia Baron has already made the same suggestion." He leaned forward and placed his palms on the desk. "If we come to agreement, there will be no more of this audience damages nonsense?"

"Not from me," Burton said.

"I will recommend to the other directors," Pearl said, "and I am sure Mrs. Baron will join me, that Tay-Sachs does not join in, and will try to discourage, such actions."

"The Pantheon Opera," Kreuz said, "depends heavily for its existence on contributions. Already ticket prices have excluded many students and other lovers of opera. Your fee must be reasonable, Mr. Gold."

"One dollar," Alexander said, "and other considerations."

"I will save my thanks," Kreuz said suspiciously, "and my apologies for the implications of my earlier words, until I hear the other considerations."

"I want complete access to the TV movies of the performance in their original form," Alexander said.

"Provided they are viewed in this building in the presence of our security people," Kreuz agreed.

"I want to be able to examine the stage and the set of the last act of *Rigoletto* before it is struck."

Kreuz looked at his watch and pressed a button on his desk. "No one will touch the last-scene *Rigoletto* set until I give the order," he barked. "Mr. Gold and his associates will examine the set shortly, as well as the backstage area"—he glanced at Alexander; Alexander nodded—"accompanied by Captain Morgan. And any other areas he wishes to inspect. Understood? Good." He turned back to Alexander. "What else, Mr. Gold?"

"If it becomes necessary, I may want a reenactment of the last act."

Kreuz looked horrified. "Do you know what you are asking? If the artists are still here, the cost—"

"I know what it costs, Mr. Kreuz; I paid for it last year at the ballet. If I need it, I get it."

"Ballet is not opera; the difficulties are tenfold."

"No orchestra will be needed." I stepped in. "Piano or recorded accompaniment will do."

"But the artists? The strain? Every time a singer performs, he shortens his—"

"They can talk through the arias," Alexander said. "But they must be in costume and move through their actions at the proper speed. The set, the lighting, everything must be the same as at the performance."

"What if they have engagements elsewhere? You cannot—"

"Would you rather have the police keep them here?" Burton said. "You'll get even bigger headlines. 'Pantheon stars behind bars. Police trying to make suspects sing.'"

"I will ask the artists. But there are limits; it cannot be forever. We have performances of *Rigoletto* on Sunday, Thursday, and next Sunday, then some of the leads will go on to other engagements and the covers will take over. Salome Auber, I know, and D'Aquilla. Brezhnikov too, I think."

"By next Friday, Mr. Kreuz," Alexander said, "or I will not need it at all."

"I will do my best, Mr. Gold. But it must be at a time when it will not interfere with preparation for another performance."

"I've always wanted to star in an opera," Pearl said eagerly. "Let me be the stand-in for Thea Malabar; we're the same size."

"The same height, maybe," I said, "but you'd never get into her costume without a shoehorn."

"They could let it out a little," she said.

"That'll be the first time they ever let a sack out at the hips," I said. That would teach her to make cracks about my left bazoom; a Norma never forgets.

"The costume can be arranged." Kreuz sounded slightly annoyed. "Is there anything else, Mr. Gold?"

"You will arrange interviews with everyone, *cooperative* interviews, tomorrow and Sunday."

"Everyone? Who is everyone?"

"The singers on stage: Rigoletto, Sparafucile, Maddalena, the Duke of Mantua."

"These are great artists, Mr. Gold. You cannot . . . They must be treated with delicacy. The artistic temperament . . . I cannot guarantee cooperation; just that they will be there. They have already given statements to the police, you know."

"I'm sure you can do better than that, Mr. Kreuz," Alexander said. "I know your reputation. If you explain that the alternative might be a thorough grilling in jail by Lieutenant Warshafsky, and a suit by the Pantheon for the damages caused by each one's part—call it accessory to a crime—in the murder of Thea Malabar, they might find it advantageous to cooperate with me."

"Yes, yes, Mr. Gold, no need to teach me. It will be as you say."

"Also the director, the Czech. Valczyk."

"He will cooperate; he is not a singer. But he was backstage with me when—"

"And last, Mr. Kreuz, you. When I have a chance. Here."

"Me? Why me? I was not on stage. I told you."

"I've been checking up, Mr. Kreuz. Reading all about your adventures. About how every opera singer you ever dealt with hates you. And more important, that you hate all singers. Especially coloratura sopranos. And particularly Thea Malabar."

18

I had sent Pearl to our office to start organizing the case files, and Burton to gather the police information. Alexander and I had gone through all the backstage technical storage areas with Captain Morgan and were now inspecting the last-act *Rigoletto* set.

From the seats in which we had watched the murder of Thea Malabar, the scene had looked completely different. Under the glare of the bare bulbs that now lit the dark stage, the dilapidated old inn on the left looked like a cheaply made fake, cheesecloth and paint, the magic all leaked out. The sinister river on the right, empty of water, was just a wooden flume lined with black plastic. It's all in the presentation, I thought, in the misdirection, in the lighting. Add to that the wish, the *need* to romanticize that lives in all human hearts. By candlelight, all girls are beautiful, all men dashing lovers. Without romance, without fancy, the human race would wither, die out. Or become less human. A real old inn, I am sure, no matter how well lit, would have looked fake. In the theater, only the fake is real.

"Let's go down into the set," Alexander said.

Captain Morgan, now in a conservative charcoal gray suit, was waiting for us at the left side; stage right, now that I'm treading the boards. He led us to the rear of the stage; upstage. The back of the flats making up the inn were solid wood, plywood painted a matte black. "To reduce the light reflections," Morgan said.

There was a sort of Z-shaped passage, walls and ceiling lined with black acoustic tile, black carpet on the floor, leading into the entrance arch to the main downstairs room of the inn. "It's a light and sound trap," Morgan explained. "Valczyk is very particular about any stray light or sound spoiling the effects onstage. He insists on absolute silence backstage, and he keeps all the lights off, except the control consoles. But no matter how hard you try, there are always tiny glows and little noises backstage; it's unavoidable. This way, almost none of it gets onstage."

"Is this the way Salome Auber, Maddalena, enters the room at the beginning of the scene?" Alexander asked.

"Everybody," Morgan said. "Sparafucile too. It's the *only* way to get into the inn from backstage. Just a few extra steps. Make a left to enter, one step and make a right, a few more steps and another left, and you're standing in the arch leading into the main room."

"It's very dark in here," I said.

"Touch the sides of the passage as you walk," Morgan said. "You can't go wrong."

The post-and-beam construction holding up the second-floor planking was real, as was the floor we were standing on. That is, the lumber was real, but the adze marks were stuck-on styrofoam. There was a shelf across the entire inside of the front of the inn, the audience side, about eight feet up, on which dozens of odd-looking candles were set. Each thick candle had a shiny metal bowl-shaped reflector behind it, and a tiny spotlight next to it.

Our footsteps rang like drumbeats on the bare wooden floor of the inn. "Is this where Gilda was killed?" Alexander asked, stopping at the middle post.

"She was leaning back against the post, head hanging forward," Morgan said, "her knees bent inside the sack. She was facing stage left, in profile to the audience, so that she could open her eyes a little without the audience seeing she was really alive."

"Wouldn't it have been easier," I asked, "more natural, if her head were inside the sack?"

"I understand that Valczyk wanted it that way, but she said she couldn't breathe, so he changed it. Actually, it looked better this way," Morgan said, "more dramatic. The candlelight catching her golden hair, reminding you, as Rigoletto enters in the last scene, that his daughter is already dead, that he is paying Sparafucile for the murder of his own daughter."

"Does he come through a light trap too?" Alexander asked.

"There's another one just downstage of the one we entered by," Morgan said. "Rigoletto and Gilda enter the scene *outside* the inn on the road parallel to the footlights, except that there are no footlights. And there's one more, upstage center, where the Duke enters, just before he goes into the inn."

"Are those three the only entrances to the set?" Alexander asked.

"Only those. No one is going to enter across the river, so that side, stage left, is completely blocked off."

"How about from above?"

"The outdoor portion can be entered from above, theoretically, but it would be impossible to do it without being seen. There were twenty-four hundred people watching, and four cameras. No way. Besides, if you're thinking about the killer getting at Thea Malabar, she was inside the main room, downstairs. The second floor of the inn was solid wood; the Duke walked on it, remember?"

"Couldn't you drop into the second floor from above, and then get down to the first floor?"

"Not a chance, Mr. Gold. All Valczyk's indoor sets have ceilings; didn't you notice?"

"Not really; I was just impressed by how right everything looked."

"Ceilings are just one part of his technique. The candles are another. Didn't they look great?"

"I wondered how he did it. Do you know, Morgan?"

"Some. These are special candles, thicker than usual, with triple wicks; give about three times the light of normal candles. The reflectors concentrate the light where he wants it, like spots. Then there are small spots at each candle, with dimmers, so he can adjust the light intensity and still have it look natural, as though the light is all from the candles. He has small air jets running next to each candle, to make the flame flicker, and to blow it out at the right time. You didn't think they went out by accident, did you?"

"I thought it was something like that. I assume that the controls for blowing out the candles also lowered the light levels automatically in the right proportions and in the right places?"

"They had a control console just for the candles, Mr. Gold. This production must have cost as much as an *Aïda* or a *Flying Dutchman*."

"It was worth it, Morgan. I'll compliment Valczyk when I see him. Now, is there any way of getting into the second floor of the inn from backstage? Through the back flat, maybe?"

"It's solid plywood. And the only way down from the second floor is the stair at the back of the main room."

"What about trapdoors?"

"Our stage has lots of trapdoors, naturally, but they're all locked. You can't even get into the area below without authorization. We can't take the chance of some million-dollar star breaking a leg because some idiot forgets to close a trap securely. But anyway, the floor of the inn is solid planking, with no trapdoors, so what's the difference?"

"Are you sure the only way to get onstage was through one of the light traps? Could the backdrop have been cut and later patched?"

"First thing I thought of, Mr. Gold. Everything was intact. And it wasn't a backdrop. Valczyk used flats, and not flimsy ones either. They were solid pieces, bolted together. Did you notice that there was no waving of what should have been solid walls, the way it is with some sets?"

"Yes, everything looked real. Could some bolts have been opened, at a corner, say, and someone slipped in, stabbed Malabar, slipped out, and rebolted the corner?"

"Those flats are walls, Mr. Gold. They support the second floor. If a corner had been unbolted, everything would have collapsed. Besides, it's a six-man job."

"What about the front of the inn? That's only black gauze with planks painted on."

"Scrim, it's called, not gauze. The wood posts are solid; they have to be to support the second floor and its ceiling. The scrim wasn't cut, couldn't be cut, without someone seeing. That side was toward the audience."

"The lights were quite dim, at times."

"If they were dim outside the inn, they were bright inside, so you could see in. If they were dim inside the inn, they were bright outside. Wherever the action was, the lighting was increased. Valczyk made it look natural, but he's very conscious of the audience; they always have enough light to see what's going on."

"I don't know; when Maddalena put out the candles, you couldn't exactly read a telephone book in the inn."

"The candle on the outside wall opposite Gilda kept her well lit."

"One lousy candle?"

"A special candle, with a reflector behind it and a spot next to it, shining right on her. You saw her well enough; I certainly did, and I was in the back of the orchestra. The glow from the fireplace showed Sparafucile quite clearly too. You may not have noticed, but Valczyk never lowered the glow of the fireplace; that would have looked unnatural. All he did was to increase the lighting outside, which automatically made the inside lighting look dimmer."

"You're a student of the theater, Morgan?"

"All my life I wanted . . . This was as close as I could get."

"Do you watch all the operas?"

"At least once. It's the main reason I took this job. Not that I see all of them all the way through; sometimes there are problems. I get into all the rehearsals too."

"The rehearsals of this one?"

"Valczyk barred even me; would you believe it? Mr. Kreuz told me not to make a fuss. But I checked out the set after final dress rehearsal; my job isn't just crooks, you know."

"So you're telling me that there was no way for the killer to get to Malabar except through one of the light traps?"

"That's the way I see it, Mr. Gold."

"How dark was it during the last act, at the time of the murder, backstage?"

"About the way it is now. I figured you'd want to see it the way it was, so I had the console lights and the control lights turned on. Of course, there were always penlights going; people had to move around. And leaks under doors, odds and ends, things like that."

"Didn't Valczyk want total darkness?"

"He's practical; he knows you can't have things exactly the way you want all the time. The unions wouldn't stand for complete darkness, either. But practically no light leaked out onstage, and that's all Valczyk cared about."

"So there was enough light to see who went onstage, who went into the light traps?"

"Oh, sure; you can't have big stars stumbling around in complete darkness."

"Did any of the backstage people see anyone going into any of the light traps who wasn't supposed to?"

"I questioned them all, twice. Nobody saw anyone, except for Sparafucile, Maddalena, Gilda, the Duke, and Rigoletto. But you got to realize, Mr. Gold, these people are there to work, not to check up on who does what. That's the job of the stage manager. He swears only the right people went in."

"How about someone *dressed* as Sparafucile?"

"In fairy tales, Mr. Gold. He would not only have to look like Sparafucile, he'd have to know the part, sing like Sparafucile, and have Brezhnikov tied up in a closet someplace. Or else meet himself coming out when Brezhnikov is going in."

"But someone *could* have sneaked into a light trap, couldn't he?"

"It's possible, Mr. Gold."

"And out again?"

"Also possible. But how would he get to Malabar without being seen?"

"The inside of the inn wasn't exactly floodlighted."

"Everybody's eyes were adjusted to the dim light. You didn't have any trouble seeing what was going on onstage, and neither did I, from the back of the theater. The cameras didn't see anything either. The way I figure it, the killer had to be one of the people onstage: Auber, Brezhnikov, or Cacciare."

"Not D'Aquilla? He swore to kill his wife, you know."

"Only if he caught her in Sicily, where he wouldn't be convicted. Besides, if you remember, Rigoletto never went into the inn."

"But if one of those three killed Malabar, how was it done?"

"I was hoping you could tell me that, Mr. Gold."

19

"In all the movies I ever saw," I said, alternating the hot peppers and the oil-cured olives between the tahini, the hummous, and the eggplant dip—all solid garlic; no way Alexander was going to feel romantic tonight—"the hero used to say, 'He only got me in the shoulder,' and five minutes later he was beating up three guys in black hats."

"That's the movies," Burton said, loading his plate. "The shoulder is really full of major nerves and blood vessels. The aortic arch passes quite closely to the right shoulder, and the carotid and brachial arteries split off just under the clavicle."

"But there was practically no blood at all," I said. "Nothing on the floor."

"The bleeding was all internal," Burton said. "The knife severed the aortic arch, the largest blood vessel in the body, right next to the brachycephalic trunk."

"But she was stabbed in the right shoulder," I said. "The heart is on the left."

"The heart is almost in the center," Burton said. "It tilts leftward. But the aorta, the main blood vessel leaving the heart, goes up and across, splits to the head and arm, then curves down again. The arch of the aorta is right under the hollow on the right side of the neck. With that cut, she certainly lost consciousness within ten or fifteen seconds; practically no blood went to the brain at all."

"I can read the medical stuff later," Alexander said. "Give me the information I need."

Burton put some of everything on his toasted pita, took a big bite, and washed it down with a giant gulp of Prior Double Dark beer before he answered. I suspect he did it as much to drive Alexander crazy as out of love for the spicy Israeli dishes.

"Thea Malabar," Burton said, "was killed by a downward stab, or thrust, of an ordinary pointed kitchen knife. It entered the hollow formed by the collarbone and the rib cage at the right side of her throat, angling inward and slightly toward the victim's back. The knife was sawed forward, severing the aortic arch adjacent to its junction with the carotid and brachial arteries. The knife was then forced in deeper, so that the handle was almost completely buried within the wound."

"Which way was the knife facing?" Alexander asked.

"Sharp side of the blade front," Burton said. "That is, Malabar's front."

"As though it had been stabbed downward from behind by a right-handed person?" Alexander asked.

"By a person using his right hand," Burton corrected. "Although there is no reason the left hand couldn't have been used. It was not necessarily a downward stab either, in the classical downward-stabbing technique, with the blade coming out of the bottom of the fist. Don't forget, Thea Malabar was sitting on the floor, slouched against the center post. If the killer was standing, he could have slipped the knife in with the blade at the front of his hand, like a swordsman."

I stood behind Pearl and tried that position. "It's a bit clumsy that way."

"Let me get down on the floor," Pearl said.

"Yes, it's easy that way," I said. "But it could also have been from the front too, either left or right hand. Or even if I were on her right, like this. Or her left." I tried each position. "Actually, with her sitting on the floor, it's easy to stab her there from any position, with either hand."

"Was the knife recently sharpened?" Alexander asked.

"It was a brand-new knife," Burton said, "with a seven-inch blade. No trace of its having been used for anything. And it had been sharpened to a razor edge and point."

"That proves premeditation," Alexander said.

"Even the police," Burton said drily, "never considered this a sudden crime of passion."

"Why stab her there?" Pearl asked. "I never heard of anyone being murdered by stabbing in the shoulder. Not even on TV."

"It worked, didn't it?" Burton said. "The killer had to know anatomy, that's for sure."

"The sack," Alexander said. "It was the only place he could have stabbed her without tearing the sack, without the knife showing or blood staining the sack Gilda was in."

"What difference would that make?" Pearl asked. "She was certain to be discovered in a few minutes anyway. As soon as Rigoletto slit open the sack, he'd know she was dead."

"Wait a minute," I said, closing my eyes, seeing the whole thing. "I know who did it and how it was done. Burton, did the medical examiner determine exactly when she died?"

"Between the time she was put into the sack and the end of the opera."

"Very funny; I knew that without the little black bag. Doesn't matter. Visualize this: Rigoletto drags the sack toward the river with his right hand. He hears the Duke singing. He stops, holds the neck of the sack with his left hand, and, with his back halfway to the audience, cuts open the sack on the side away from the audience. He drops the dagger and pushes the sack down to Gilda's shoulder. He steps forward with his left foot and pushes the sack down a little more with his left hand. There's a big flash of lightning; everybody is blinded. Not Rigoletto, because he's expecting it, and anyway, he's looking down. His body shields the view for several seconds, during which he slips the knife into Gilda's shoulder with his right hand. Nobody sees a thing. He hides the sawing motion with his sack-pushing motions. He sings an aria, then he runs to the inn and bangs on the door. Everybody is watching him. Gilda is dying, but nobody sees; a classic example of misdirection. By the time Rigoletto gets back to the sack, Gilda is gone."

They were stunned; finally Burton spoke, slowly. Grudgingly, I would say. "I suppose it's possible. But the police checked all four videotapes, and they didn't see D'Aquilla kill her."

"Naturally," I said. "If we didn't, the cameras didn't either. They were all at the back, anyway. He had the motive too; she was unfaithful to him from the first month they were married. That's very serious for a Sicilian; everybody knew he had sworn to kill her."

"But only in Sicily," Pearl said.

"That's because killers of unfaithful wives don't get the chair in Sicily," I reminded her. Not in New York either, but why becloud the issue? "He knew she would never set foot in Sicily, and devout Catholics can't get divorced, so when he saw Valczyk's dim lighting, and her, helpless in a sack at his feet, he knew he could get away with it."

"This is all conjecture," Burton said. "Where's the evidence?"

"I just thought of something else," I said. "The reason D'Aquilla shoved the knife all the way in was so he could act surprised later, when she didn't sing. If he left the knife handle sticking out, he'd have to explain why he didn't see it right away."

"Why didn't she scream when he did it?" Pearl asked.

"Maybe the knife cut her windpipe."

"It didn't," Burton said.

"Then maybe you can't scream if you have no blood pumping into your brain; I don't know. The shock? Maybe she did make some noise, moaned, but the music covered it. Let's check the audiotapes at that moment."

"I'll check," Burton said, "but when is that moment?"

"I can't prove it," Alexander said. "I can't prove anything yet, but I have a feeling it wasn't done that way. There are too many risks; one little slip and there'd be two thousand witnesses to the murder. Plus four cameras."

"*Could* it have been done that way, Alexander?"

He thought for a moment, but there was no way out. "From what we know now," he ground out reluctantly, "yes."

Well, at least he was honest. "Do you have a better solution, Alexander?" I asked. "Any solution?"

"No." *Very* reluctantly.

I was magnanimous, as usual. "All right. I won't go to Zacharias and Warshafsky yet. I'll bet if we check the videotapes closely, looking specifically for this, you'll find I'm right."

"We'll check the tapes," Alexander said. "Burton, will you arrange it? After the interviews, tomorrow. But it doesn't feel right; there has to be another . . ."

Yeah. Anything but me. No man is a hero to his valet, and no wife is *allowed* to be a hero—except for cooking, maybe—to her husband.

20

"D'Aquilla is *stunato*," Carlo Cacciare said. "Very crazy. After this season, I never work with him again."

Cacciare's dressing room could have served as his fan club's headquarters. Every horizontal surface was loaded with photos of Cacciare with presidents, dictators, queens, kings. Change that. Loaded with photos of kings and queens *with* Cacciare. Every picture showed the kings, and especially the queens, looking worshipfully at Carlo Cacciare. I didn't know if this came about through artistic retouching, cropping, or careful selection, but wherever he looked, he could be reassured that the great shakers and doers of the world, and especially their wives, were thrilled to be in the presence of the greatest of them all.

The walls were not neglected. Except for the mirrors, and there were *lots* of mirrors, every square inch of wall was tapestried by four-foot-wide hangings of black velvet—for easy transport, I presume—to which were pinned photos of women with Carlo Cacciare, gazing adoringly at Carlo Cacciare, kissing Carlo Cacciare, hanging onto Carlo Cacciare's arm. Famous beauties, not-so-famous beauties, not-so-beautiful beauties, downright homely beauties, young, very young, middle-aged, old, and very old, it didn't matter; they were all there. The pictures were pinned, not glued, to the velvet. Sensible. To make room for new ones, you'd have to put away some old ones; after all, there was only so much space on dressing room walls, unfortunately. Some of the women made no effort to conceal their wedding rings; some did. A few wore engagement rings; it made no difference to Cacciare. They looked at him and he looked at the camera. There were even pictures of pictures, clipped from today's paper. Dozens. But only those with Cacciare in them. After all, what else on earth was there more worthy?

"What is so crazy," I asked, "about being angry at the man who is having an affair with your wife?"

"Angry, yes. Is okay," Cacciare said. "But to want to kill? Over a woman?" He shook his head.

"What about *your* wife, Mr. Cacciare? Wouldn't you feel like killing the man who seduced her?"

"It cannot happen, *signora,*" he said. I braced myself for a lecture on how, when one has tasted the nectar of the gods, mortal food is insipid. "She is up on the mountain; no man could come near her. Always two servants with her all the time. And one man, he will kill the servants if a man say even *bon giorno* to my wife. And her too." He smiled securely. "Is for honor."

"You seem very insecure," I said, bravely controlling my natural instinct to tear his ears off *first.*

"Is experience," he explained. "Women are not think, women are feel. Cannot help. Two sweet word and . . ." He shrugged, helpless to resist the gales of primal passion that ever roared around him. Useless, my questioning him now. I would figure out how to get him later. With a look, I turned him over to Alexander.

Alexander, knowing what I wanted him to do, pulled his

chair up real close to the great lover and put on a fierce face, crowding Cacciare back into his chair. "Why did you kill Thea Malabar?"

"I? No." Cacciare pulled further back into his chair. "I am upstair. Sleep."

"You were sleeping? When you had to sing 'La Donna è Mobile' in a few minutes?"

"No, no. Duke of Mantua sleep. I am ready, always. Professional."

"And when Maddalena went upstairs with the candle, did you see any blood on her hands?"

"Blood? No. No blood."

"So you killed Thea Malabar after that. You sneaked downstairs, killed her, then sneaked up again."

"No, no, is not possible. Too much light down the stair."

"Only one candle, Cacciare. And everybody was watching Rigoletto, outside the inn."

"Not candle only. Valczyk have light."

"You still could have done it, Cacciare, crouched over low."

"No. I don't do. Ask Salome Auber."

"She'd lie. She's in love with you." Alexander was bluffing.

"Of course, yes, but she not lie. Not for jail. We—" He stopped suddenly.

"We what, Cacciare? Talk to me or I'll tell the police how you could have done it."

"We . . ." He stiffened. "A gentleman must not say."

Insane. Behind a transparent scrim? In front of two thousand people? One beam of light and the price of any unsold tickets to the next performance of *Rigoletto* would go up ten times. Twenty. Valczyk would go down in history as the master of realism, and twenty contraltos would fight, kill, to get the role, each announcing to the press that she would sacrifice anything, *anything,* for her art, while humming a few bars of "Vissi

D'Arte." Tenors are known to be crazy, sopranos even worse. But Salome Auber was a contralto. And married. I was looking forward to a long talk with Salome Auber. A long, interesting, *informative* talk. Meanwhile, now that Alexander had softened Cacciare up, it was time for me to take over.

"You and Salome Auber," I asked, "you're old friends?"

"Last year. From Nice. On the boat."

"The yacht? Zacharias' yacht?"

"La Belle Hélène. Like the opera. Kreuz make arrange. End of season, take me home to Napoli. Good food, drink."

"I thought the idea was that the principals would get together with the director and work out the general way the opera would play."

"Yes, also." I guess that in Cacciare's mind, the important thing was a ride home on a yacht, free. "I know already Kerfiu, Malabar. Work together ten time."

"That was the first time you met Salome Auber? Had you seen her since?"

"Only that time. And now. Yes, first time. Right away she like me."

"And Thea Malabar didn't object? I heard you and she . . ."

"Only when work together one time. Why she object? She have Zacharias."

"With Mrs. Zacharias on board?"

"If Helen Zacharias let Malabar on boat, for why? To play bridge? She also must have friend, you don't think so? Is Helen make decide who come on boat; is her home, no?"

"Who? Kerfiu? Valczyk?" Then a thought struck me. "You?"

"No me," he said virtuously. "Only one lady a time. Also she is too big. Very nice lady, but . . ." He shrugged, consigning all ladies over five foot eight, his height, to eternal deprivation. I wondered what he thought of me.

"So who was her boyfriend, Carlo? Valczyk? Kerfiu?"

"Must be Kerfiu; Valczyk no sing good." Freud was wrong, claims Carlo Cacciare, living proof that the libido connecta to de earbone.

"Did you see evidence of this, Carlo?"

"No have time, but who else?" The pair of them must have come up for air about once a day.

"How did you get along with Kerfiu?"

"Kerfiu okay. Rumanian, so not *great* singer, but okay."

"Nicholas Kerfiu was one of the greatest bassos in the world."

"Good, yes. But only Napolitano can be *great*. Is natural; in Napoli, everybody sing."

"Did he say anything about Helen Zacharias? His relationship with her?"

"Kerfiu not say about women. Gentleman, you understand."

"Did Valczyk say anything? About Mrs. Zacharias?"

"Only *Rigoletto*. Crazy. Talk, talk, talk. Light, costume, set. Walk fast, walk slow, walk with music. Why? Nobody come for watch walk. Come to hear sing. Opera is sing, no? Not walk. Everybody come hear Carlo Cacciare sing."

"Minos Zacharias says his wife killed herself. What do you think?"

"What else he can say? *He* kill her."

"He couldn't have killed her; he wasn't on the yacht at the time."

"I think you right; I no remember see him. Also, Greek no care if wife is *putana*. You know story *Phèdre?*"

"Italian opera is full of unfaithful wives."

"Only story. *Phèdre* is true. With own son of husband."

"So you think Helen Zacharias did kill herself?"

"No. *Putana* never kill self. Husband must kill."

"And if it wasn't Minos Zacharias?"

"Could not be Salome." She must have been pinned to the

bunk like a butterfly. "So was Thea Malabar. Kill wife so can marry Zacharias."

Time for Alexander to take over again. "Did it bother you to work with Ettore D'Aquilla? That he was the hero of the opera?"

"D'Aquilla not hero. Have lead role, yes, but only *tenore* can be hero."

"Did D'Aquilla threaten you?"

"All time. Say if I come to Sicily . . . Ha! I *never* go Sicily."

"Then why did you appear with him?"

"Kreuz. He explain. Cost me half million. Dollars. What I can do?"

"Why did you sign the contract in the first place?"

"Three year ago. D'Aquilla not want kill me then."

"You mean, in all these years, you and Thea Malabar—? Less than three years ago?"

He spread his hands. "Always I am busy. Very busy."

"Did D'Aquilla threaten to kill Thea Malabar? In your presence, I mean?"

"Oh, sure. All time. But she don't go near him alone. He know if he kill her in America, they kill him. She is American, you know."

"Do you think Americans would be more likely—?"

"Oh, sure. Everybody know. If he kill *putana* wife in Sicily, is big honor, okay. In America, is not allow."

"Are you saying D'Aquilla would not kill Thea Malabar in America because he would be punished?"

"Oh, sure. What good kill her if you die too? Ha?"

"Then who did kill her?"

"D'Aquilla."

"But you just said—"

"He know how. Nobody see. Siciliano know how do."

"But he was never inside the inn. How did he do it?"

116

"I am Napolitano. I do sing. Only Siciliano know how."

Dead end; try another road. "Why did Salome Auber hate Thea Malabar?" Alexander's shot in the dark, I'm sure, but why not? We hadn't gotten a thing worthwhile out of Cacciare yet.

"Everybody hate Thea Malabar. She make trouble every opera. More for women. She hate all women, so women hate her."

"Did she ever do anything specific to hurt Salome Auber?"

"All time. Never let Salome on same opera. Too beautiful. Cost Salome plenty money, plenty famous."

"They worked together on this opera."

"Kreuz too smart. Bring Salome for make Thea look bad."

"Kreuz hated Malabar?"

"Oh, sure. Everybody."

"You too? But I thought you and she . . ."

He shrugged. "You hate, but you sing together. So . . ." I'd have to ask Pearl how that works. I guess the catalogs don't cover everything you can learn at the conservatory.

Alexander asked, "Could Salome have killed Thea Malabar?"

"Only *before* she come up stair." He was most emphatic about that. So much for chivalry.

"Of course, if you and she were working together—"

"You think I'm a *stupido?* I want to kill, I tell *woman* to help me? *Singer?* Ha!"

"What about Sparafucile?" Alexander asked. "Gregor Brezhnikov?"

"He's a Russian," Cacciare explained. "Could do anything. Sparafucile is *assassino,* no?"

"Did you see him do anything suspicious?"

"All time. Always look to see who watch him. And very bad act. Too much arm up here. Like so. Verdi is Italiano, beautiful. Not Russian. Valczyk have much trouble with Brezhnikov."

"And Malabar? Did she have trouble with him?"

"All time. She want Valczyk throw him out. But no can do. No more big singer free now."

"Why didn't she like him?"

"Maybe Brezhnikov tell her no? Not allow say no to Thea Malabar."

"You did, evidently. For many years."

"I am Cacciare. But I never say no. Is insult to woman. Just too busy."

"Would Brezhnikov kill over something like this?"

"He's a Russian. Crazy. Maybe he think Malabar is commissar of opera, can send him back. Who can say?"

"Did you hate Malabar enough to kill her?"

"Not *real* hate; just hate. Not to kill. Only D'Aquilla want to kill. I tell you before. D'Aquilla. He's a Siciliano."

21

"**W**ould you believe . . ." Alexander asked. "In this day and age?"

"Opera is a small, closed world, Alexander," I said. "Look at it as a foreign culture."

"If they're all like Cacciare—"

"I'm sure they're not," I soothed him. I was also sure each one we interviewed would be . . . unconventional in his own way. And why not? Life would be very dull if the limits of human behavior were contracted. Someday, not in the middle of a case, of course, I would ask Alexander to describe himself as seen through the eyes of Carlo Cacciare. Do him some good. Then again, maybe it wouldn't. I'm learning. Two years ago I would have said, "I think Carlo's kind of cute, don't you?" just on general principles. Now I just changed the subject. "Do you think he did it?"

"He's still on my list," Alexander said. "Nobody can be that much of a . . . a walking testicle and live. That had to be an act. Opera singers are, after all, actors, so it would come easy."

"It jibes with what we know about him from the computer."

"Of course it does. The computer can only print out what's public knowledge, what's recorded. You think he doesn't have a public relations man controlling what gets on the record?"

"I'm sure he does, Alexander. But that doesn't mean it's not true. He is in the public eye constantly; it would be impossible to fake everything."

"Politicians do it; why not opera stars? But I'm not saying what we saw isn't real. I'm saying there must be more to it. He's hiding lots of things."

"Naturally, Alexander; you didn't expect a complete biography in one interview, did you?"

"Well, then, what's he hiding? There may be some information, some clue, that will break this case wide open, that he's not telling us about, covering with his talk about women. My God, I'll bet he hasn't read a single book in twenty years."

"There are lots of people in this world, Alexander, who haven't, with much less reason. I'm more interested in the things he said. Did you notice how easily he accused others of killing Helen Zacharias? First Minos, then Malabar?"

"Yeah, and they were good choices too, but he didn't do it rationally. With him it was just instinct. Based on personality, relationship. Whoever he doesn't like is a potential killer."

"Rational isn't the only criterion, Alexander."

"It's the only one whose results you can be sure of. He was also sure that Kerfiu was having an affair with Helen Zacharias because he sang better than Valczyk."

"Not because he sang better, but because he was a singer. Evidently all Valczyk wanted to talk about was theater technique. Any woman would have understood why Helen would pick the singer."

"Why assume she was having an affair with either one? With anyone?"

"That can be analyzed rationally. Remember what Helen Zacharias said? What Minos told us? I don't recall the exact words, but it was that she and Minos had an understanding. Thea Malabar, his longtime mistress, was on board. Minos had escorted his wife and Thea to public events before, so Helen knew and approved, or at least didn't object to her husband's mistress. Under those conditions, she must have had a lover or two herself, particularly if Minos and Thea were together on the yacht. She would do it; any woman would understand, even if she didn't feel like that."

"Agreed, but that doesn't mean she had one there. Or that it would be either Kerfiu or Valczyk."

"Yes, it does. If it was a short trip on an ocean liner, Helen might pick the captain, or some other officer. But on their own ship? She would never have an affair with a crew member. Remember what Minos said about appearances? Employee attitudes? No, it had to be a guest. And if we believe our super-tenor, Cacciare was indisposed. So it had to be Valczyk or Kerfiu."

"It could have been Cacciare; he doesn't necessarily always tell the whole truth. But it didn't have to be anybody."

"It certainly did, Alexander; you'll never understand women if you live to one-twenty. The one time Helen would *have* to take a lover, or have it *look* as if she did, was when Minos had his mistress around. Even if she wasn't in the mood, she had to have a man courting her."

"All right," he grudged. "Maybe. Look into Kerfiu's death, just in case it wasn't an accident. Maybe Minos was jealous."

"I did already; heart attack in his home. Nothing in the slightest way suspicious."

"Then why did you bring it up?"

"I didn't . . . Drop it. The point is, with a lover, especially with a new lover—"

"How do you know Kerfiu was a *new* lover? Or Valczyk? Wasn't Helen an opera buff?"

"All arts, but all right. Even an old lover. Under these conditions, with her husband away *without* his mistress, would she have killed herself? That might look as though she did it because she missed him."

"Not necessarily, but you're probably right, especially if he was a new lover. But if it wasn't suicide, she was pushed. Not an accident. She knew the boat, she knew the sea. And she was athletic."

"Right. Suicides can't take the overwhelming problems anymore or they want to show someone how bad they feel and how much they'll be missed or want to make someone feel guilty. But to wait until her husband leaves? It doesn't fit. If you ever drive *me* to suicide, Alexander, I'll do it in front of your eyes."

"Minos Zacharias will be very happy to hear this analysis."

"He knows. You think he doesn't, Alexander? He has to prove that whoever pushed her was not doing it at his orders."

"I can't prove that; nobody can. Especially since it had to be Thea Malabar."

"So Carlo Cacciare was right again. You should trust instincts more, Alexander. Especially mine."

"The probability is, then, that Thea Malabar was killed to stop her from talking."

"Right. And what she was going to say was that Minos Zacharias told her to do it, or rather, that after she did it, one year after, she'd be all dressed in virginal white and some second-rate soprano would be singing 'Oh Promise Me.' Then she found out about Patricia Horgan and said, 'Minos, darling, if you don't (a) eliminate my husband and (b) do right by me, I'm going to have a talk with Demetrios Taramakis and will *you* be sorry.' Then Minos says, 'If you do, he'll kill you too,' and she says, 'I don't care; life without you . . .' And he says—"

"Okay, I don't need every little detail acted out, with gestures. But Minos didn't kill Thea. He wasn't on that stage."

"He wasn't on the yacht either, Alexander, but he killed Helen. Magic? Did the ancient Cretan gods—?"

"All right, Norma. He hired . . . or something, someone. But who? And how?"

A very good question. Two questions. No, one really.

22

"You're supposed to be a sixteen-year-old girl," Jan Valczyk shouted. "You *run* out of the house and *throw* yourself into your father's arms. Float, like a feather. With the music."

The plump lady on the stage turned with dignity and addressed the director. "Mr. Valczyk, I have played Gilda five times in the past thirty years, and I've always—"

"Then you've been doing it wrong for thirty years, Anna." Jan Valczyk took a deep breath, then, in a soft voice said, "All right. Walk. Don't run. But it must be in rhythm with the music. Like a dancer. Let me show you." He got up and whispered to us, "I'll be with you in a few minutes." He ran to the stage, looking more like a page in his orange Day-Glo jumpsuit and baseball cap than an internationally famous opera director.

Alexander and I watched, fascinated, as Valczyk positioned himself and nodded to the pianist. After a bar of music, he ran lightly to downstage center, tapping his high Cuban heels exaggeratedly on the floor with every beat of the music. "Like so," he said, smiling gently. "You can do it, Anna. I will give you taps on your shoes too." He signaled to the wings. A young man came out and knelt at the singer's feet.

"This is humiliating," she said. "My shoes—"

"No, no," Valczyk soothed her. "Just a temporary aid. By tomorrow it will be instinctive to move with the music. Only plastic taps and gum. Pull them off yourself when you feel ready. You be the judge." He dashed off the stage to rejoin us.

"It is surprising," Valczyk said, "how many great singers have no appreciation of the visual aspect of opera. To them, the sound is all that counts; appearance is of little importance. Yet, by the use of taps, when you turn movement into sound, they find their musical instincts will not permit them to move off beat."

"Is that why you wear this outlandish costume?" I asked.

"I am so pleased you understand, Mrs. Gold." His accent was more British than the queen's. "The visual shock catches their attention, helps them comprehend that opera is for the eyes too. And I too wear taps, metal ones, on all my shoes"—he lifted one foot—"so that I too move in harmony with whatever sound there is; my own speech, if nothing else. Unconsciously, the singers begin to move with the music like dancers. Then everything works for the audience, almost a ballet, even though no one realizes why." He smiled boyishly and turned back to the stage. "Good, good," he yelled. "You see, Anna? Okay, let's take a break. Back in an hour. Third act." He motioned us to follow him out of the auditorium. "Let's find an empty office so no one knows where I am. I'm sure you want no distractions."

In the uncarpeted corridor, we found ourselves talking and walking in rhythm with the metronomic beat of Valczyk's clicking heels. I had no trouble; Valczyk was almost my height, but Alexander's pace was much shorter, so I took Valczyk's arm to shorten his step. He understood at once, and matched his walk to mine.

"Is that why they say you treat all performers like puppets?" I asked. "The taps, I mean?"

"It's not just the taps," he said. "I insist that everyone does everything exactly as blocked out in rehearsal. I spend a lot of time and money getting the effects I want exactly right, and if a singer isn't in the right place at the right time, nothing works. Actors and singers think—I know, I was an actor in London once—that they are the play, but they're wrong. No singer has ever seen a scene in which he performs; only the director can see the opera as a whole. If a singer can't, or won't, do what I want, I replace him."

"Even if he's the star?"

"There have been times I was replaced instead, when I was younger. Not entirely coincidentally, I think, none of these plays were successful. Knowing that, the actors pull in their horns."

"You also wrote a dissertation on Oriental puppetry," Alexander broke in. "Surely that had something to do with your reputation."

Valczyk's craggy face broke into a smile. "I'm sure it contributed but, I assure you, I do listen to actors. But I make the decisions. When I was an actor, I found myself disagreeing with the director so often that I decided I was really a director at heart. I was drawn to puppetry—no back talk there—and in the process of getting my doctorate in Dramatic Arts, I traveled through the East, studying puppetry in each country I visited. But puppetry is too limited, so I started working in the theater again. Someday I'm going to try film."

"I'm sure you'll do very well there," I said, as we found an empty office.

In his glaring Day-Glo outfit, Jan Valczyk looked more like a comic-strip cowboy than a world-famous Central European director, more at home in the bulldogging ring than in the Pantheon Opera House, but having experienced the magic he had worked with *Rigoletto,* I ignored the rough-cut appearance and addressed the sensitive and brilliant artist within. "We have to question you about the murder of Thea Malabar," I apologized, "and the questioning may seem tough to you, Mr. Valczyk, so before I start, I must tell you how much I enjoyed the production and the way everything worked so perfectly."

"Thank you, Mrs. Gold," he said in his exaggerated British accent, although with him I didn't mind, since I knew he came to it by way of a Czech teacher. "It is so good to be appreciated by people who understand."

"I'd like to add my admiration for the perfect timing and coordination of all the elements," Alexander said, uncharacteristically, "as well as the technical innovations. The administrative difficulties must have been immense, especially in dealing with the prima donnas. Of both sexes."

Valczyk flushed with pride, as if he understood how rarely men like Alexander give compliments. "Actually, the leads were much less trouble than the backstage people. They're all real professionals and, other than a tendency to upstage each other and to milk applause, they cooperated beautifully."

"I thought you'd have trouble with Carlo Cacciare," I said.

"Not really. He's almost perfectly typecast as the Duke of Mantua. I gave him an outstanding costume and very high heels, made sure he was better lit than anyone else onstage at the same time as he. You may not have noticed, since I didn't use spots, but he always had strong direct lighting, and a bit of backlighting to give a halo effect, as though the Duke was glowing with an inner light, which, for the audience, added to the appearance of his rank. I then took Polaroids of the first dress rehearsal and showed him how he stood out, how handsome he looked. He understood that if he gave me no trouble, he would outshine Rigoletto."

"You knew of his trouble with D'Aquilla?"

"Of course. Gossip in this business spreads with the speed of light. Actually, I made use of the hatred D'Aquilla had for Cacciare."

"I noticed," I said, "there was a strong undercurrent of tension, antagonism even, between Cacciare and D'Aquilla."

"Good. I was hoping it would come across. When the Duke calls Rigoletto a buffoon and warns him he is going too far, Cacciare is talking to D'Aquilla. And when Rigoletto swears vengeance on the Duke, it is D'Aquilla swearing vengeance on Cacciare."

"Wasn't that dangerous?"

"Not in the slightest; they were never alone together. But even if they were, D'Aquilla would not dare do anything here. Crimes of passion, defending your honor, are not legitimate defenses for murder in the States."

"Yet D'Aquilla's wife *was* killed."

"Rigoletto was never inside the inn."

"*Assuming* Gilda was killed inside the inn." It was not the time to bring up that I had figured out how D'Aquilla could have killed Gilda outside the inn. "Rigoletto was offstage for a long time while Gilda was in the sack. Plenty of time to sneak into the room through the light trap and do it."

"Anyone could have sneaked into the light trap leading into the inn, though the chances are he would have been seen by one of the backstage people, but how do you get to Gilda? It's a good twenty-five feet from the arch to the post where she was sitting."

"The light was pretty dim inside the inn."

"It was light enough to have her fully visible all the time; to point up the irony of Rigoletto enjoying his revenge while we see his daughter dead. I had all the inn lighting on the front wall, on a shelf, so the audience could see clearly. And when there was any action inside the inn, I turned up the inside lights a bit more and had a cloud pass over the moon, darkening the outside, so that the inside appeared even brighter. No one could have walked, or even crawled, across that stage without being seen. And taped."

"Then how was she killed?"

"The first thing I thought of was that someone had cut a trapdoor in the floor, unbeknownst to me, and used it. But I checked later; it was one solid mass of wood."

"How about loosening a plank, lifting it to stab her, then renailing it the next day?"

"The police checked the floor right after the killing. Every plank was firmly nailed. Lieutenant Warshafsky seems to be very thorough."

"When I spoke to Captain Morgan, he agreed that it was impossible, that there was so much support below the floor, and so little room, that no one could have crawled through there. And she was stabbed on the audience side of the stage, which would have easily been seen. Besides, her head was down; anything coming from below, she would have noticed."

"Not necessarily; her hair was over her face. But I agree with Morgan; it seems impossible. If you do find out how it was done, please let me know. I may be able to use the technique. In a play, of course," he added, smiling wryly. "Have you seen the videotapes yet?"

"Later today, but since Captain Morgan and the police have checked all four and nobody's been arrested yet—"

"I'd like to see them too, if I'm permitted. I know this opera backwards; it's possible I'd catch something you'd miss."

"I'm sorry," I said, "you're a suspect. It took all of Hugo Kreuz's influence just to let *us* see them. Let's go on. Did you have any problems with Salome Auber?"

"Just the usual jealousies. She resented my making her up with garish makeup, claimed I was trying to make her ugly on Thea Malabar's orders. I told her she was playing a prostitute and she had to look the part, but if she felt she looked like a prostitute in her everyday face, I would be glad to announce to the press that here was another example of perfect typecasting by the artist's own admission."

"You should have been a diplomat," I said. "How about Gregor Brezhnikov?"

"He was the most difficult of all. Six months ago he played Sparafucile at the Bolshoi. Their style is heavy declamation, like old-fashioned movies. He tried very hard to stop chewing the scenery, but he still hammed it up more than I wanted. Was it very noticeable?"

"Not too bad. His intensity really came through. Did he hate Cacciare or D'Aquilla?"

"I thought I was imagining it, but now that you mention it, yes, I think both. Not just them either. I think he hated—although it might have been fear—Thea Malabar too. The only one he seemed to get along with was Salome."

I could see that Alexander was chafing at the bit, so I let him take over. "Where were you," he asked, "at the time of the murder?"

"Backstage," Valczyk said. "Stage right. I had been standing in the back of the orchestra until the middle of the last act, then I went backstage."

"Near the light traps?"

"Of course. After the Duke enters, center rear, all entrances and exits are made stage right."

"Did you see anyone going in, or coming out, who shouldn't have been there?"

"No, but you must realize that wasn't my main interest at the time. I think I spent more time near the monitors and the consoles than at the traps."

"Was there anyone at the entrances *all* the time? The stage manager, for instance?"

"He was there off and on. He only goes to the entries when someone is ready to go onstage."

"Then what were you doing there?"

"Nothing, actually; although in an emergency, I would be available. I served my apprenticeship years thoroughly, and I can do almost anything required backstage, including running the light consoles. But I was really there to wait for the end, near the downstage trap; that's the only way to get to the front of the scene. We all, Edelstein, Kreuz, and I, would have taken bows with the leads. That is very important in the theater; practically the only public recognition we get. It also has great economic value."

"You weren't wearing this clown suit, were you?"

"Oh, no, we were all in white tie and tails. Most dignified."

"Kreuz was with you all the time?"

"Off and on. We exchanged a few words. Do you suspect him too?"

"Right now, everybody's a suspect. I thought you insisted on absolute quiet backstage; no talking."

"Are you thinking of my taps, or my conversation? First of all, absolute quiet is as unattainable as absolute darkness; we do the best we can, that's all. Second, it is possible to make very little noise, even with taps, if you walk very slowly and carefully. Third, the light trap is carpeted, so anyone could walk in there without being heard. And last, I don't wear taps on my dress shoes, only on my work shoes."

"The floor of the inn is bare wood; like a drumhead."

"I wanted to emphasize the action inside the inn. It was very effective, I think. The Duke going upstairs. Sparafucile's steps of doom, the struggle when he stabs Gilda, the dragging out of the sack. There was the resonance of Gilda's knocking on the door when she sacrifices herself and Rigoletto's pounding on the door when he discovers Gilda has been killed, with the sound of the steps on the inn's floor. I didn't do it just to make your life difficult, Mr. Gold. And, as I said, you can walk silently on any surface, if you do it slowly and carefully enough."

"But somebody did kill Thea Malabar. Right in front of two thousand people and four cameras. And nobody saw a thing or heard a sound."

"Misdirection, Mr. Gold? The way a magician does? He carefully directs your attention to one action while performing another right as you watch. In Prague, when I was a boy, I loved watching magic shows. All boys do, I am sure."

"You can't misdirect a camera, Valczyk. And certainly not four cameras." Alexander thought for a moment, then shook his head, looking disgusted. Or maybe frustrated. "How well did you know Thea Malabar, Mr. Valczyk?"

"Quite well. We had met several times socially, in Europe, spent a week together on the Zacharias yacht, and, of course, we worked together on *Rigoletto*."

"Did you ever have an affair with her?" I guess, if you have to ask the question, there is really no delicate way to put it. For Alexander, at least.

"No. Actually, I think her reputation was somewhat exaggerated. As far as I could tell, she was interested only in Minos Zacharias."

"I understand that she and Zacharias had split some weeks ago, so he was no longer an impediment."

"I make it a practice not to get involved with performers. Can you imagine my problems directing both Thea Malabar and Ettore D'Aquilla if I ever had?" He smiled at the idea.

"Not Salome Auber either?"

"A very beautiful woman, but no."

"I understand she and Carlo Cacciare—"

"There are many rumors about Cacciare," Valczyk said. "So many that I sometimes wonder if he does not encourage them himself. This notoriety has certainly helped make him the most expensive tenor in the world and will, no doubt, sustain him when his golden tone fades away."

"So that left you and Helen Zacharias at loose ends on the yacht."

"We had three fantastic hours to ourselves after her husband left but, unfortunately, that pest Nicholas Kerfiu kept coming between us. And so disappointing was my wooing that she killed herself rather than face another hour with me." He suddenly dropped the bantering tone and spoke seriously, sadly. "It was . . . was silly of me to joke about . . . But your suggestion . . . Helen Zacharias was a wonderful woman, loved by all. We were all shaken by her death."

"Not loved by all, that's for sure, Mr. Valczyk."

"The rumor that she was pushed overboard? I've heard that said. But who? Why? If there was ever anyone in this world who had no enemies, it was Helen Zacharias."

"Minos Zacharias never wanted her dead?"

"Never having been married, I do not speak from experience, but I do observe carefully, and I believe there are many times in a marriage, it is almost inevitable, husbands wish wives were dead, and vice-versa. That does not mean they act on these impulses, which soon pass and allow life to go on again."

"Minos Zacharias is a man of action who has the ability, the money, to order almost anyone's death. He, naturally, would make sure to be somewhere else at the time."

"As I said, Mr. Gold, I am a careful observer. Helen was an exceptional woman, very beautiful. She could have modeled for the Venus de Milo. A natural athlete, swimming, diving, water skiing, sailing, skiing, tennis; she was good at anything she touched. A gifted pianist and a patron of the arts. I believe that Minos loved his wife, and even liked her."

"You sound like her press agent."

"I didn't mean to imply that she was an angel," Valczyk said. "She was a tough businesswoman who could hold her own with her husband and his associates. Her father, in fact, was grooming her to take his place when he retired, or died, and made no secret of it. And had she ever decided to enter the profession, I would have shown you a *Medea* that would have resounded for years. She was a perfect match for Minos Zacharias. He would never have hurt her."

"Thea Malabar *didn't* hurt her?"

Valczyk thought for a moment. "That, yes. I believe that did hurt her. That and being childless. She really loved children; supported an orphanage in Athens all by herself. But Zacharias couldn't—you must have read about it—so she took it in stride. Her husband's little philanderings . . . they were unimportant. Everyone in that set did it. But his love affair with Thea Malabar—from the first year of their marriage—that, I think, really troubled her. She never showed it, you understand, never said anything. She treated it as a sickness her husband had, an incurable disease they both had to live with."

"If she accepted Thea Malabar, why did she kill herself?"

"I'm not so sure she did, but if she did, it wasn't over Thea Malabar."

"Could Minos have told her, just before he left, that he was going to divorce her to marry Thea Malabar?"

"Anything is possible, but I do not believe it."

"Could it have been an accident?"

"Highly unlikely. Helen knew the sea, knew her yacht. She had good balance, good reflexes. No, an accident is even more improbable than suicide."

"Murder, then?"

"Again, no. How is easy. But who?"

"Thea Malabar," Alexander said bluntly.

"She's the most likely, of course."

"Why 'of course'?"

"Thea is—was—a woman without morality, conventional morality. She read, believed, her own publicity. She believed her fans, believed even the claques her manager arranged, presumably without her knowledge. She felt she was a goddess, above human standards, restrictions, laws. She did what she wanted, lived as she wanted, took what she wanted. It was all her due."

"You didn't like her?"

"It was stronger than that, Mr. Gold. I actively *disliked* her. But so did everyone else her life touched. Only Minos Zacharias liked her, and I'm not too sure . . . Now that you ask, I don't think Minos really liked her. He may have been obsessed with her, fascinated by her, even loved her, in a way, but like? Thea Malabar was not likable."

"So you think she killed Helen Zacharias?"

"No, I don't, I'm sorry to say. Not herself. She was accustomed to having things handed to her on a silver platter. And why should she kill Helen Zacharias? To marry Minos Zacharias? A year has passed, and there was no sign that I could see of their coming marriage. In fact—" He stopped suddenly.

"Patricia Horgan?"

"Again, a rumor. But yes, I think so. If Thea did it, she must have known she'd be the prime suspect. With all her faults, Thea was not stupid."

"Then who?"

"I've thought about it many times. Nothing fits."

"Tell me what you know," Alexander said. "How it happened."

"We were sitting in the salon, Thea, Helen, Kerfiu, and I, sipping brandy. Salome and Carlo were off somewhere by themselves. Helen had sent the steward away. At about ten, Kerfiu excused himself to go to bed, saying he was tired.

Shortly after, Helen, who had drunk a bit too much, went on deck for some fresh air, a walk around. About fifteen minutes later, Thea went out too; I assumed, to talk to Helen. She came back shortly after and announced that Helen was not in a mood to talk to her, and she was going to bed." He hesitated, then said, "This is all in the magistrate's report, Mr. Gold. Wouldn't it be more helpful if you read it firsthand? I may make some minor slips of memory."

"What you're saying is good enough for my purposes, Valczyk. Go on."

"Very well. I walked Thea to her cabin, then took a turn around the deck myself. I didn't see Helen, so I assumed she had gone inside, but when I passed her cabin, there was no glow of light. I finished my walk and felt—I don't know what exactly . . . something odd. The timing was wrong. So I knocked on Helen's door. No response. I knocked again, then opened the door. The bed was still made and the door to the bath was open. Now I was really alarmed. I went to Thea's cabin, thinking maybe Helen was there, but Thea was alone, getting ready for bed. She slipped on a gown and we went back to the salon. It was empty. I told Thea to walk counterclockwise around the deck and I went clockwise. No sign of Helen. I went to the bridge and told the watch. He woke the captain. They checked the log and retraced the route, all lights on, all hands looking. They found her scarf, so we knew we were in the right place. But Helen was gone."

"From what you just told me, doesn't it look to you as though Thea Malabar had pushed her overboard?"

"Yes, but it doesn't fit. Thea was not a woman who lived by the standard morality, but she would not commit violence. Poison is possible, but unlikely. Thea's tongue was her most fearful weapon."

Alexander's antennae went up at the mention of poison.

"Could Helen's drink have been poisoned? Not necessarily a fatal poison, just a sleeping pill? To make her lose her balance?"

"I think we would have noticed if anyone . . . Helen refilled the glasses herself, and none of us were sitting close to each other. I've thought of all these things too, replayed that evening many times. There was nothing suspicious; nothing."

"Helen Zacharias *was* murdered," Alexander said stubbornly. "It has to be."

"Why are you talking about Helen Zacharias?" Valczyk asked. "Kreuz told me you were investigating the murder of Thea Malabar."

"The two are connected," Alexander said. "How, I don't know yet, but they are."

"Mr. Gold," Jan Valczyk said gently, "they may be, for all we know, and they may not be. But Helen Zacharias died a year ago, thousands of miles away. Nicholas Kerfiu is dead. Thea Malabar is dead. You are relying on my memory, which is very good for scenes but not absolutely perfect; on the statements of Minos Zacharias, who will tell you only what he wants you to know; and on the love-blinded eyes of Salome Auber and Carlo Cacciare. If what you believe is true, would you not be better off to concentrate on the death of Thea Malabar, which we know for certain was murder, and then see if there is a connection with the death of Helen Zacharias?"

Good advice, real good advice, but wasted. Once Alexander gets an idea into his head, nothing can get it out. Not even facts. Him with his "has to be." And if I said I agreed with Valczyk, that would not only prove to Alexander that he was right, it would also prove that I was against him. Either way, good-bye case.

23

I had made up my mind not to even mention the murder of Helen Zacharias, so as soon as we left Jan Valczyk, I said, "So Thea Malabar did it, right?"

"It looks like it, but as Valczyk said, she wasn't stupid. It would have been smarter to do it when Minos was on board."

"Then *he* would have been blamed. You can't marry a dead man."

"There would be no way to prove anything. Even with an open-and-shut case like that, Malabar wasn't charged."

"Demetrios Taramakis doesn't need fingerprints. The only reason that Minos Zacharias is still among the living is that he was not on board the yacht that night. So Demetrios Taramakis killed Thea Malabar. Or, rather, had her killed. That's why you kept insisting the two murders were connected."

"It was obvious. Didn't you read the computer printouts?"

"If you would pick up your own dirty underwear, I'd have as much time to read as you. Who do you think—"

"You want a maid, I'll get you—"

"I don't want anyone else living . . . My cleaning woman and the service are enough." Alexander never questions what I spend. Doesn't even know. By him, bookkeeping is women's work. Thank God. But I don't even like him thinking about how I run the family, so I gave him an opening. "So you think Demetrios Taramakis bribed someone—one of them—to kill Thea Malabar?"

"Not necessarily bribed, although money may have entered into it. How do you bribe a Carlo Cacciare? Or a Jan Valczyk?"

"Cacciare could have been bribed with Salome Auber; he seems to really like her. Auber could have been bribed with a *Carmen,* or a *Norma* with Joan Sutherland. Valczyk could have been bribed with a theater, a company of his own, even the Pantheon. Kreuz could have been bribed by *not* throwing him out of the Pantheon; by giving him a life contract. Brezhnikov could have been bribed, or threatened, rather, by *not* getting him sent back to Russia."

"And Ettore D'Aquilla? How would you bribe him?"

"He'd be the easiest. All you'd have to do is show him how to kill his unfaithful wife in front of two thousand people and get away with it."

"Naturally. So how was it done, Norma?"

"I did the heavy thinking, Alexander. You can take over the technicalities now." I mean, what else are the filthy little beasts good for, anyway?

24

"I give him a medal," Ettore D'Aquilla said. "I make a party. Big party, everybody come. Lotsa wine, lotsa good food, big cake. Everything. Music, dancing, very happy. Everything."

"You wouldn't be ashamed to honor your wife's murderer?" I asked.

"Ashame? Sure. I ashame I no do myself. But okay. Why ashame? She's a *putana,* no? You think I like people say I'm a *cornuto conténto?* My wife is *putana* and I no care? I a laughing, ha, ha, my wife is *putana* and I no care? You crazy?"

"I don't mean you shouldn't care," I said. "But to celebrate?"

"Yes, to celebrate. I kiss his hand, I give him present. You tell me who do, I take him to Sicily, make big parade. In Palermo. Come meet my mama. My mama say to me, 'Ettore, no marry this woman. She have bad eye. She have bad heart. She is not a Siciliano. She is too young. You want marry nice Siciliano girl, I find.' But I no listen to my mama. First month, maybe first *week,* I don't know, I trust . . . She . . ." He shook his strong gray head. "I teach her sing; I teach her *breathe.* And she—"

"You made her what she is today," I said sarcastically.

"Sure," he said. Sarcasm is wasted across language barriers. "When she come to me she is nothing. Skinny like bone. No diaphragm. No head tone. No vibrato. No coloratura. Nothing. I teach. I make. I show. She say she love me. Okay. Make announce. I take her, meet everybody, arrange. Make audition. I say, you want me, you take her. Everybody do. I'm a big star in Italia, even that time. Not big like now, but big. Then we get marry. Everything finish. Everybody laugh at *cornuto.* Say D'Aquilla is *cornuto.* I no kill, so everybody say *cornuto contènto.* I must tell all newspaper, she come to Sicily, she come to Italia, I kill. But she not come. Too smart. I teach too good. My mama say I'm a *capados;* next time you listen to the mama."

"So you figured out a way to kill her in America?"

"I? How I kill? I no in house."

"When you cut open the sack you used a real dagger."

"Sure. Must, to cut laces. Not sack, sack too hard. In back side is laces, easy cut. Cut with right hand, hold sack with left hand. How kill?"

"After you cut open the sack, the lacing, I mean, you stand with your back to the audience and pull open the sack. That's when you kill her. With your left hand."

"How I get knife? Why she no make a scream?"

"The knife was in your left sleeve. You held the sack over her mouth. You didn't have to silence her completely, just enough to have her drowned out by the music."

D'Aquilla looked around. "No. I have no blood. No fingerprint. Police examine. Very careful. Nothing."

"You had a handkerchief around the knife, held in place by a rubber band. You took the handkerchief off after you killed her and disposed of it after the performance. Maybe to an accomplice. It was at least twenty minutes before the police came."

D'Aquilla took a deep breath, thought for a moment, then

said, quietly, "You know, you a very smart lady. Why you no tell me this ten year ago? You tell me, I kiss you. Thousand times. But you wrong. In Sicily, even in Milano, I kill her. Yes. No trick, just kill. But not in America. I smart for music, not for kill people. You think I know how make like you say? Even if I *very* smart, you think I *stupido?* Do when everybody look? Take picture? No. You say I do. Why? I hate? Sure. *Everybody* hate. She not just *putana;* she lie, she steal, she kill. You want smart? Valczyk, Kreuz. You want hate? Auber, Cacciare, Brezhnikov. Yes, Brezhnikov more as me. You think I kill when open sack? Ha! Brezhnikov kill with *spada.* Everybody see, but is okay. Is *suppose* to kill. She make scream? Okay, is *suppose* to scream. Why you not ask Brezhnikov? Ha?"

Another good theory shot to hell. Well, I *would* ask Brezhnikov; let him get out of this one. Meanwhile I gave Alexander a look; I had nothing more to ask. Right now.

"When did you first realize, Mr. D'Aquilla," Alexander asked, "that Thea Malabar was dead?"

"After curtain. When she no sing, I think, Ha! Valczyk make trick. When *l'assassino*, Sparafucile, kill, no come back alive, sing. Valczyk always do funny thing. You know tap on shoe? Make noise?" Alexander nodded. "So. Is good Gilda no sing. Is more natural, you understand?"

"Is there any way you can prove this? Any evidence, Mr. D'Aquilla?"

"Prove? No. How I prove? Yes. I prove. If I know she dead, you think I sing 'Non morir, mio tesoro'? No! I sing 'Happy, Happy, thank you, God.'"

"That's not quite proof, Mr. D'Aquilla. If you had killed her, you would have behaved exactly the way you did."

"So. If I kill, I do this; if I no kill, I do this. No?"

"A good point, Mr. D'Aquilla. It makes me wonder if you are really not smart enough to figure out that if you kill your wife onstage, it would appear so foolish that no one would think you would do that."

"That I understand. In opera is more foolish than that. What I say . . . I no know *how*, you understand?"

"Possibly someone showed you how to do it?"

"Why somebody do that?"

"Someone wanted Thea Malabar killed, but was not in a position to do it himself."

"You think I'm a *assassino*?"

"You wanted to kill her; you were in a position to do it. Someone wanted her dead and was not in a position to do it. He could plan it; you could execute it. A perfect combination."

"Mr. Gold, better you talk with Mrs. Gold. Maybe you smart, but not right way. If he want kill Thea, why he must onstage? Why he tell me? I do stupid mistake, police catch, I tell police on him. And. If I do how he say, he come to me, say, Give money, keep shut the mouth. Every week. Ha! Every day. I no smart, but I no crazy."

"He wouldn't dare blackmail you. You could tell the police he was an accomplice."

"Ha! Who believe? He lie, say no. How I prove? No. To kill, must do by alone."

"There's one man who is smart enough to figure out how to kill Thea Malabar, who you could be sure would never blackmail you."

"Absolute sure? For my life? *Impossibile*. Who is this man?"

"Demetrios Taramakis."

Ettore D'Aquilla considered this for a moment. "Okay. Is the man. *One*. But I never know. Never meet. I swear on my mother. You understand what means?"

"I understand, Mr. D'Aquilla. And I do believe you never met Demetrios Taramakis." Alexander led me to the door and let me out first, then turned to D'Aquilla and said, quietly, "But that doesn't mean he didn't do it through an emissary. Or that you didn't kill Thea Malabar."

25

"You knew all the time," I told Alexander as quietly as my clamped teeth would let me. "You let me make a fool of myself in front of Pearl and Burton. You even agreed with me that Rigoletto could have killed Gilda the way I described."

"Why not?" he said, reasonably. "It was certainly possible."

"Why not? Because it was more likely that Sparafucile could have done it. And easier."

"Not necessarily. It would take very fine coordination to stab Gilda in the breast with his right hand, horizontally—fake it, I mean—while stabbing her in the right shoulder with his left hand, vertically."

"But Maddalena threw a heavy canvas over Gilda's head and held her arms."

"Which made it even more difficult. Further, despite the loud music, if Gilda had screamed—"

"She did scream."

"I mean really screamed, off-key, Maddalena would have heard it."

"She did really scream. It was chilling. Whatever you can say about Thea Malabar, she was a great actress."

"I meant a second scream, Norma."

"There was no second scream. At least that I could hear."

"Exactly. So either Sparafucile and Maddalena were working together, or Sparafucile had to time his stabbing, both thrusts, for the exact moment Gilda screamed. That would take some coordination."

"Not necessarily, Alexander. Opera singers are used to working in rhythm with the music. Remember Valczyk's putting taps on the new Gilda? Anna Whatshername? Maybe Sparafucile poked Gilda with his sword—I'm sure it was dull—in rhythm with the music, as a cue to scream. That way he knew exactly when to kill Gilda with his left hand. And Maddalena would never know it. While he was stuffing Gilda into the sack, Maddalena is going around saving money by putting out the candles."

"Not all the candles. There is still the one at the center of the exterior wall of the inn. We could see Gilda clearly."

"Sure. Not moving, head down, hair in front of her face. Could have been dead for hours, for all we know."

"I still think it wasn't done at the time of the stage murder. How much easier it would have been for Sparafucile to kill her *after* he put her against the post. That way he wouldn't have to worry about Maddalena seeing him do it. He could even have done it with his right hand while holding the sack with his left hand. It would look like he was tightening the sack around her head."

"You may be right, Alexander. But why do you—? Are you sure Sparafucile did it?"

"Not yet, but who else could it have been?"

"Maddalena. After she put out the candles, before she went upstairs to the Duke, she stopped at Gilda for a while and bent over. Like checking to see if everything was all right. And her back was to the audience."

"I didn't notice that. Are you sure?"

"Positive. You were watching for Rigoletto to come in, that's why. Maddalena had a candle in her right hand to light her way upstairs. That way, she could have slipped the knife in with her left hand and no one would see."

"I do remember her waking up the Duke. He reached for her and she blew the candle out."

"Yeah. And then they did—whatever they did—if they did. Crazy."

"All actors are crazy, Norma. Didn't we have something like that in the Boguslav case?"

"That was different. Nobody could have seen a thing, even if the lights went on. This was real death-wish stuff. I read that some people, monsters, get all excited by killing."

"It might have happened that way, but I don't see Thea Malabar as a sex-thrill victim. I still think the murder ties in with the death of Helen Zacharias. But if you're right about Salome Auber, I have a feeling that Carlo Cacciare is involved some way."

"The two of them? Salome and Thea, fighting to the death over that plump little peacock? Come on, Alexander."

"No, it's not that way, obviously. I just don't want to count out anyone yet. Let's see what the videotapes tell us."

I knew what they would tell us. Nothing. Zilch. Else why would all our suspects be walking around loose? Ah well, at least there'd be no commercials.

26

"**G**o back to camera three," Alexander said. "I think I saw something there."

"We've gone through this act three times with each camera," I said. "Aren't you getting a little bored?"

"It's just been from the time Gilda goes into the inn to when Rigoletto starts to sing the finale. Only six minutes."

"Yeah, but six times twelve is seventy-two minutes. What are you going to see a fourth time that we didn't see the first three times?"

"I saw *something,* I'm sure. Let's do it this time with the sound off. It'll help me concentrate better. Morgan, tell the technician to increase the contrast a bit more. I wish we had a bigger screen."

"With a bigger screen you lose detail, Alexander," I said. "This size monitor is the best compromise. If we had brighter light on the stage—"

"There's enough light for the special lenses," Alexander said. "The trouble is this damn resolution we have on American TV. If we had the same number of lines per picture the Europeans have, we could enlarge the picture twenty percent and still see everything clearly."

The picture appeared on the screen again; Gilda entering the inn, Maddalena throwing the canvas over her head and holding her arms, Sparafucile stabbing Gilda with his sword. Not perfectly clear, but good enough to show that Sparafucile could have stabbed Gilda with his left hand. Not did; just could have.

Sparafucile put Gilda into the sack Maddalena was holding. Gilda was completely limp. Dead already or just good acting? It might have been possible for Maddalena to see the end of the knife in Gilda's shoulder; and then again, with Gilda's long hair covering everything, it might not. When Sparafucile dragged the sack to the middle post and leaned Gilda against it, her head moved limply, the hair swinging in front of her face. Again, good acting? Sparafucile went to the fireplace and sat facing the door, waiting for Rigoletto.

Maddalena finished putting out the candles and, holding her own candle, went to Gilda. With her back to the audience, Maddalena bent over Gilda, at least fifteen seconds, and did something, impossible to see what. Maddalena was halfway up the stairs, the candle in her left hand, when Gilda's head turned left, toward Maddalena. Voluntary, or a death spasm? Again, we'd never know. Maddalena stopped for a second, then continued upstairs. The light from the remaining candle on the front wall made flickering shadows across Gilda's hair.

Suddenly Alexander yelled, "Stop. That's it. Back up a few seconds." The screen went blank, then the scene was repeated. Two seconds after Gilda turned her head, Alexander said, "Here. Stop here. Now go back one second. Watch Gilda's head carefully. There! Did you see it?"

"See what, Alexander? I didn't see anything."

"Do it again. Watch. There. Now did you see it?" I shook my head. "A tiny flash, Norma. A glint. Look once more. Do it again."

This time I saw it, whatever it was. So short; so small.

"Alexander," I said gently, "the candle was flickering. Also the candle in Maddalena's hand as she walked upstairs. Lenses pick up reflections."

"No," he said stubbornly. "Go back. Freeze that frame." The operator flipped the frames forward, one by one, until Alexander said, "Stop. That's it. Look at it, Morgan. Is that a lens reflection? Isn't it more oval than round? Almost vertical?"

"Well, it could be, Gold," Captain Morgan said. "And then again, it could just be the flicker of a candle or a stray bit of light."

"It's right at the side of her head," Alexander persisted. "The exact spot."

"So's a lot of blond hair," Morgan said. "A few strands caught a flicker of light as her head moved—"

"I know that's the knife," Alexander said.

"Then why does it show up on only one camera for one frame only?"

"That camera was the only one at exactly the right angle, and the knife was moving."

"So was her head, Gold. No one keeps perfectly still, ever, and the candle flame was certainly moving too."

"That was the reflection off the knife," Alexander said firmly. "Show it to Warshafsky, he'll tell you."

"Even if I do," Morgan said, "and I will," he added hurriedly, "what will it prove? Can you imagine taking this into court? All it proves, *if* it was the knife, is that Auber or Brezhnikov didn't do it. But from the way you described everything, Brezhnikov is as likely a suspect as we've got."

"It was the knife," Alexander muttered. "It has to be."

Again with the "it has to be"? No "it's obvious"? It was obvious to me that Alexander didn't know anything definite, or even highly probable. "If that was the knife, Alexander," I said, "who was holding it? The Invisible Man?" I could have cut my tongue out; I didn't mean it to be sarcastic, it just came out that way.

Alexander stood up. "That. Was. The. Knife." he said, neck swollen with anger. I reached into my bag and got the bottle of nitro pills I always carry. "Put this under your tongue, darling. Sit down." He obeyed quietly. The angina must have hit hard for him to give in this quickly.

"All right," I said. "We'll work on two assumptions: that it was the knife and that Brezhnikov didn't do it, leaving us only five suspects. Four without Salome, or else it was a trick of light, and Brezhnikov is still the most likely killer. Let's analyze it tonight with Pearl and Burton."

"If it was the knife," he said, after the minute was up, "Cacciare couldn't have done it either."

Unless he was in cahoots with Salome Auber, I said to myself; this was no time to get Alexander started again. Which left us with four suspects again. Better than six? Or three? Not in my book. By me, two is too many.

27

"**D**o you really think," Burton asked, "that Demetrios Taramakis is behind the murder?" Pearl had been researching all day, so I forgave her the cold supper. Not that she had turned up anything important, but the hacked chicken with sesame-peanut sauce wasn't too bad. Not perfect, naturally; it could have used some garlic and a touch of chili oil, but Pearl is afraid to deviate from recipes. So I suffer in silence.

"It certainly looks like it," Alexander said. "I can't see any of our suspects killing Malabar this way for the fun of it. Talk about doing it the hard way: this was a public execution in spades. Remember what Minos Zacharias said about appearances? Well, if anyone had the idea that Taramakis was getting soft in his old age, this shattered his illusions, but good."

"Can you imagine what it took"—Pearl's eyes were opened wide—"what it took to force one of the world's greatest opera stars to kill the world's greatest soprano onstage, right in front of everybody?"

"Not just singers," Alexander reminded her. "Directors and general managers too. I haven't cleared Valczyk or Kreuz yet."

"Even so," Burton said, "it sounds a little crazy. If you're going to persuade, or worse, force someone to commit murder in such a theatrical way, the last person you'd pick is an opera singer. They're crazier than dancers, even the low voices."

"They're just high-strung." Pearl Hanslik, defender of the weak and helpless. Ha! She should see how they throw their weight around. "It's a very demanding field. A singer's whole life depends on the health of two little pieces of tissue. A tiny sniffle is a major disaster."

"From what I hear," I said, "an even greater disaster is when some other singer gets his name above yours in the ads."

"Well, of course," she said, "The biggest stars make the most money and get the best roles. The better singers *should* get the star billing."

"The best public relations guy," I corrected, "and the biggest claque, you mean."

"Now that we've finished the important discussion," Alexander said, "can we get back to the trivia?" He glared at me. Not at Pearl, naturally. He turned back to Burton. "If he wanted to make his point in killing Thea Malabar, by having her killed onstage, who else could Taramakis pick but one of those six? A stagehand? A dresser?"

"Why do you include Valczyk and Kreuz, then?" Burton asked. "They weren't onstage. They couldn't even go onstage during the performance. Not in white tie and tails, they couldn't, and there were no supers milling around in this act."

"Those two could go anywhere and do anything without being questioned," Alexander said. "That's why. I'm not saying you're wrong, Burt; just keeping the door open."

"They *couldn't* go onstage," I said, "and I don't see general managers, or directors, who are also executives in every sense, killing someone onstage."

"That's your new theory of crime?" Alexander said sarcastically. "Look for the guy who fills out his income tax return with 'Occupation: Murderer'?"

"Don't be funny, Alexander. I mean that executives don't do *anything* themselves; they get others to execute for them. And they don't look for the hardest way to do it, either."

"So you want to eliminate Kreuz and Valczyk?" he dared me. "Right now?" I wouldn't answer that stupid question; why should I get the blame for messing up a case? After ten seconds, which is the most Alexander can hold himself in while analyzing a puzzle, he said, "Can we please get back to reality? Please?" That "please" was an "or else" if I ever heard one, so I let him talk. He waited for a moment, daring me to say something, but what's the use of my talking if nobody listens? Finally, he turned to Burton. "Do the police agree that the light on the third camera's tape was the knife?"

"They still don't know," Burton said. "The trouble is the resolution of the TV isn't good enough. When they try to enlarge that frame, the light starts getting less and less sharp. It could have been a knife and it could have been a reflection of a flicker of candlelight on a strand of blond hair."

"But the police haven't ruled out that it might have been a knife?" Alexander was grasping at straws.

Burton nodded. "They can't do that, for sure."

"Anything new from the autopsy? Any new clues? Do they have any information we don't have?"

Burton shook his head. "You know everything they know. But I must tell you, Alex, they don't buy any connection between the death of Helen Zacharias and the murder of Thea Malabar."

"They're wrong," Alexander said. "I'm more convinced than ever that the two are tightly connected."

"Evidence?"

"Not yet, but I'll get it. I still have three more interviews left tomorrow: Brezhnikov, Auber, and Kreuz. Something has to turn up."

"Alexander," I said, "wouldn't it be better if, in the interviews, you concentrated on—"

"No," he said. "Positively not. When I get the evidence that Thea Malabar killed Helen Zacharias, then I'll know who killed Thea Malabar."

Oh, boy, are we in trouble. It used to be that he'd say, when he figured out *how* the murder was done—he *is* a good technician, even I'll admit that—he'd know *who* did it. *Now* he's going to figure out, long distance, *very* long distance, who killed—that's *if* she was murdered—Helen Taramakis Zacharias a *year* ago—which her husband doesn't want him to do—and which a Greek magistrate said was an accident, so he can make somebody—one of the world's greatest singers—admit that Demetrios Taramakis—whom Alexander wouldn't know if he bit him—that one of the richest men in Greece, hired him, the singer—or her—to kill Thea Malabar, the world's greatest coloratura soprano, on a stage in front of two thousand people, four cameras, Lieutenant Warshafsky, and Alexander Magnus Gold, himself. Alexander is going to *make* him, or her, or them, admit not only that he, she, or they *killed* Thea Malabar, but *explain* to Alexander—*nobody* explains *to* Alexander; *he* explains to *everybody* else ("it's obvious," remember?)—*how* he, she, or it did it. I'm out of breath. Well, at least this time we couldn't lose any money; Alexander didn't bet anyone anything. We'd even make seven thousand dollars plus a thousand expenses. Gross. All that could happen was that Alexander would *plotz* if he failed to solve the case. And get another heart attack. Which would be all my fault. Naturally.

28

"**F**or why you want make me trouble?" Gregor Brezhnikov asked. "I not have enough from Russia?"

"You made the trouble for yourself," I pointed out, "when you murdered Thea Malabar."

"I? No. Can not be." He looked genuinely shocked, like a good actor. "Is opera. Not sharp on sword." Brezhnikov was pacing up and down like an irritated bear.

"Not with your right hand," I said; "with your left hand."

"No. You ask Salome. She say I not do."

"She couldn't see what you were doing because of the canvas she threw over Malabar's head."

"Look television picture. You see."

"You had your back to the audience, but the TV shows you were moving your left arm as though you were stabbing Malabar."

"Is crazy. How I can prove not?" He licked his lips. "Police. They say I not do."

"They're just playing with you. As soon as they're ready, they'll arrest you."

"No. Is America. Must prove."

"For a criminal trial, yes. But to send you back to Russia?"

"No. Not to go back. I die, not go back."

I didn't enjoy picking on a refugee, but he *was* a murderer and I *was* a private eye, so it was even, sort of, praiseworthy.

"Why did you hate Thea Malabar?" Alexander asked.

"Hate? Who say I hate?"

"We have witnesses, Mr. Brezhnikov. You want to tell me your side, or do I tell everything to the police and the immigration authorities?"

Brezhnikov stopped pacing and sank into a chair. "What you tell? I not do bad. Nothing."

"It isn't a question of what you actually did, Mr. Brezhnikov." Alexander was fishing, I could tell. "But what Thea Malabar would tell them you did."

"She lie!" Brezhnikov exploded. "Big lie. I not do."

"As you said before, Mr. Brezhnikov, how do you prove you didn't? Would the immigration authorities believe you? The police? The CIA?"

That struck a nerve. To someone who has been brought up on *Pravda,* the CIA has to be worse than the KGB. "CIA?" Brezhnikov whispered. "You know CIA?"

"Not personally," Alexander said, as though this was above even his ambitions, "but my wife's partner's husband"—Russians are used to long chains of influence—"is very close friends with a high official, a deputy vice-chairman of a department."

Brezhnikov looked behind himself nervously, then addressed me. "You go, Mrs. Gold. Tell partner husband I not spy. I go be American, why I be spy? I tell CIA everything. Okay?"

"What would an opera singer know," Alexander asked, "that the CIA would be interested in?"

"I not politic, you understand? But opera singer go by reception, party, dinner, all time. Is plenty big official with wife. Wife, all wife, like opera singer; very culture. Talk. I hear plenty. I tell CIA, okay? Not make trouble from Malabar, okay? Malabar big lie. Very bad lady."

"You could have given Malabar what she wanted."

"No. I never. Wife come soon, next year. With children. All arrange. What I want little skinny bad lady?"

"Salome Auber isn't skinny. She's the most beautiful woman in opera."

"Yes. Very nice. But I not do. Who say I do?"

"You didn't because Salome was having an affair with Carlo Cacciare. You were jealous of Cacciare."

"I? Jealous? Is to laugh. Ha, ha." Right out of the silent movies.

"And Thea Malabar was going to tell your wife, wasn't she?"

"What tell? Is nothing happen."

"Even if that were true, what would stop Thea Malabar from telling your wife you had an affair with Salome Auber?"

"Wife not believe. Everybody know Malabar big lie."

"Even if your wife knew that, and she couldn't, one look at Salome, and any wife would believe anything," Alexander said. "And to top it off, Malabar threatened to tell your wife that *she* had an affair with you also, and that you asked her to divorce her husband and marry you. What wife could doubt that?"

"Gold, you crazy. Is not true. But even if is, how you can know?"

"I'm a detective," Alexander said. "I have ways of finding out. The only thing I don't know yet is why she was threatening you with everything in the book."

"She want me, is why. Like say before."

"Mr. Brezhnikov," Alexander spoke very politely, "that's a lie. I'm not saying she wasn't attracted to you, or didn't want to have an affair with you. But, given her reputation, one affair more or less meant nothing. Less than nothing, if the rejection were not made public. You weren't going to tell anyone you refused her, though I'm not so sure you did refuse"—at this Brezhnikov winced slightly—"and she certainly wouldn't tell. So all this pressure, all those threats . . . what did she really want from you?"

"Money also." Brezhnikov sounded desperate. "Plenty money."

"You've just clinched it, Brezhnikov," Alexander said. "Thea Malabar did not want money. Not only did she have more than you, she could have gotten ten times what you could have given her from Minos Zacharias." Brezhnikov started to say something, but Alexander quickly stopped him. "I know they had a falling out, but there is no doubt he would have given her any money she needed. So what could it have been that she wanted from you?"

"Nothing." Brezhnikov was visibly agitated. "You go. Now." He stood up and looked Alexander over. "You go now," he repeated threateningly. I reached back and grasped my little gun. I wasn't afraid he would hurt Alexander; big as Brezhnikov was, Alexander could tear him apart with one hand, but because Alexander is so short, and looks fat, Brezhnikov might start up with Alexander, and the exertion might bring on another heart attack.

Alexander responded quietly, thank God. "Sit down, Mr. Brezhnikov. You can't afford to even touch me. Not only will you be on your way back to Russia in a week, but what I just figured out will be in the papers, and in the hands of the police, in an hour. So just sit down." In the face of Alexander's quiet dominance, Brezhnikov lumbered to his chair. "I'll tell *you*," Alexander said, "what Thea Malabar wanted from you."

"How you can know?" Brezhnikov asked in a beaten voice. "You not can know."

"Let's analyze this." Alexander leaned back in his chair, his voice taking on the Talmudic lecture tone. "What does Gregor Brezhnikov have that Thea Malabar could want? Money? Nah, we know it can't be money. His fair white body? She already got that, in spite of his protests about how pure he is, otherwise she wouldn't have dared to threaten him so viciously. Even a refugee who's been here only a few months wouldn't fear her phony accusations—spying, fooling around with Salome Auber—unless she had something firm to back up her threats." He turned to Brezhnikov. "What did she have, Gregor? Audiotapes? Videotapes?"

Brezhnikov clamped his mouth shut and glared at Alexander.

"No matter," Alexander said casually. "What annoys me most is that you have such contempt for my intelligence." This, I knew, was true. My husband can forgive any sin but this one. "Such contempt as to expect me to believe that a healthy, relatively young man such as yourself, who knows practically no one in this city, for four months rejects absolutely the persistent advances of one of the world's greatest artists—who can advance his career like lightning—and one of the most renowned sirens in the world. And you would have me further believe that this wealthy, famous, glamorous super-sexpot would keep throwing herself at you—you're not bad looking, but you're not all that great either—keep throwing herself at you for four months, being continuously rejected, when she could have had her pick of half the men in New York? Frankly, Gregor, I find that a little hard to believe. Do you believe it yourself, Gregor?" Alexander asked politely.

No answer, but Brezhnikov's look made my right hand sweat on the grip of the gun. "So," Alexander went on, "what could it be that Thea Malabar wanted so desperately, that only Gregor Brezhnikov could give her? And that no one else in New York could give her? Obviously, it had to do with the opera, with

Rigoletto. So why didn't she ask Carlo Cacciare to give it to her? Or even Salome Auber?"

He was toying with Brezhnikov now, confident he was right, slowly increasing the pressure. Brezhnikov was tense, staring at Alexander fixedly. I eased the little gun out and held it behind my bag. Brezhnikov was big and muscular; he might be fast too.

"Maybe it wasn't something Brezhnikov would *give* Thea Malabar; maybe it was something he would *do* for her. Something only a man could do, so Salome was out. But what about Carlo Cacciare? They had once been lovers; they were still friendly. What could Gregor Brezhnikov do that Carlo Cacciare could not do, or do properly? Why, just look in the mirror, Gregor. You're ready to kill me right now, and if we were alone, you might even try. When I accused Cacciare of murder, he just told me he wasn't stupid. So the only question is, Who did she want you to kill?"

"Nobody, Gold"—through Brezhnikov's gritted teeth. "Is lie. She dead. Not can prove."

"Obviously," Alexander said, ignoring the outburst, "she wanted you to kill Rigoletto, her legal husband, Ettore D'Aquilla. He was the man who stood in her way of marrying Minos Zacharias. He was the man who would not, could not, divorce her. He was the man who said, publicly, that if she set foot in Italy, any part of Italy, he would kill her. For her, it was a case of self-defense. First."

Brezhnikov took a deep breath, then another. Though still flushed, he started to take control of himself. "I be singer, Gold, not kill people. Not can prove. Nothing. Stop talk. Go way."

"In a minute, Gregor. I'm almost done. So you pretended to go along with her scheme. What plan she figured out, I don't know yet. Clearly, it was imperfect; otherwise, why would she need you? You could see it was doomed to failure—you play chess, I'm sure—and that you would be the fall guy, take all the blame. You'd go to jail or even be sent back to Russia. She might even find it convenient to turn you in herself, just to get rid of a nuisance. If you tried to implicate her, she'd just deny it, or even admit it; it's no crime to tell your lover you wish your husband were dead.

"And even if you succeeded, Gregor, even if you got away with it, you'd be Thea Malabar's slave for life. Who would she order you to kill next? What were you to do? Obvious. Figure out a safe way to kill Thea Malabar, of course. Now you had no threats hanging over you, no CIA, no immigration. You could live in America, an opera star, happily, with your family. Perfect. So you figured out how to kill her; you *did* kill her, and you thought you were safe."

"Gold"—Brezhnikov was breathing easily now—" you wrong. You ask Salome. Not can kill Malabar when Sparafucile kill Gilda. Look TV. Look my left hand. I hold Salome right hand. She say she kill Malabar. Say she scratch Malabar eye. Out. I not make bad opera. I hold Salome hand."

This didn't stop Alexander for a second. "I never said you killed Malabar when she first entered the inn. That would have required perfect timing, and it risked your being seen by Salome Auber. No, you killed Thea Malabar when you dragged the sack over to the post and leaned her against it. You spent some time, at least ten seconds, balancing her against the post and ten more adjusting the sack around her neck. Your back was toward the audience. I checked the videotapes. Nothing you did could be seen; but from behind, your motions are exactly right for the murder."

Gregor Brezhnikov looked at Alexander with intense hatred. "I not do," he said firmly. "Not can prove."

"I'll prove it," Alexander said, getting up to go. "Now that I know it's you, I'll find the proof. If it's there, I'll find it."

If it's there. But what if it isn't there? And, even worse, what if Alexander's analysis was wrong? I couldn't put my finger on it, but I sensed there was a hole in his reconstruction. At least one.

29

"**Y**ou did a great job with Brezhnikov," I told Alexander in the corridor, and I meant it too, "building a whole case out of practically nothing, just a word and a hint."

"Anyone could have done it," he said, with false modesty. "It was obvious. Once I realized that Sparafucile had the opportunity and the time to do practically brain surgery on Thea Malabar, everything fell into place; the background, I mean. Why else would a Russian defector, who had never sung with her, want to kill Thea Malabar? Did you see his face? Practically a signed confession."

"But it's really all conjecture, isn't it, darling?"

"It fits," he said stubbornly. "Perfectly. He had plenty of time. He had the motive. And the means? A knife up his sleeve? No problem."

"What made you so sure Brezhnikov had an affair with Thea Malabar? I got the impression he had his eye on Salome Auber."

"Of course, who didn't? But Salome was busy with Carlo Cacciare, so he had to take second best."

"I still don't see Malabar, who was supposed to be pretty

shrewd, picking a Russian opera singer, of all people, to kill her husband."

"She probably got the idea from the opera, the role. Sparafucile is a professional killer. In the second act, Rigoletto asks Sparafucile how much to kill a nobleman, meaning the Duke of Mantua, who is Carlo Cacciare. Malabar latched onto this because she *felt* like killing Cacciare for fooling around with Salome instead of her, which she had to read as a big insult. Then, in the last act, Maddalena suggests that Sparafucile kill Rigoletto instead of the Duke. That gave Malabar the idea of using Brezhnikov to kill D'Aquilla so she could be free to marry Zacharias. But Brezhnikov also learned from the opera. Sparafucile agreed to kill the first person who came into the inn before midnight instead of his intended victim. That first person was Gilda. Thea Malabar. A perfect fit."

"Do you really believe that Gregor Brezhnikov, who, even though he isn't a tenor, doesn't seem too bright, figured out, all by himself, how to commit a murder in front of a whole audience and get away with it?"

"First of all, he hasn't gotten away with it; I've nailed him cold. Second, just because a man can't speak English well doesn't mean he's stupid. Considering that there's a bunch of KGB men with every troupe that leaves Russia, it takes *some* brains to get away. Plus a lot of guts."

"I didn't mean it that way, Alexander. Just that it's harder to function in a place where you don't have full command of the language and the customs. And, even if he's a basso, most singers are not intellectual giants."

"Tell that myth to Beverly Sills, Regina Resnik, Risë Stevens, and a hundred others, but okay. How big a genius do you have to be to figure out, in rehearsal after rehearsal, that you have a perfect opportunity to commit a perfect crime? Or that, for self-preservation, your only solution was to kill Thea Malabar? Where would *you* have Brezhnikov kill her? In her bedroom, after the maid has taken his hat and gloves? In her dressing room in front of her dresser? In the *Eclair,* over coffee and Opera-torte? No. Onstage was the *logical* place to do it. As far as all by himself goes, what's so hard about seeing that the only time he could kill her safely was when she was in the sack? Literally. No waving hands, no struggle, nothing. She was helpless. The only problem was *how* to kill her. If he cut her throat, she might bleed all over his shoes, and good-bye perfect crime. The only way, the right way, was the way he *did* do it."

"What happened to your theory, like when you accused Ettore D'Aquilla, that Demetrios Taramakis figured out how to do it and had an agent approach the potential murderer with an offer? If you were Taramakis, would you want to use Brezhnikov?"

"No," he admitted. "Too uncertain, too risky. But more important, as far as Taramakis knew, Brezhnikov had no motive to kill Malabar. I'm sure Taramakis knew about Brezhnikov's affair with Malabar, but he couldn't have known about her using Brezhnikov to kill D'Aquilla. No, D'Aquilla was the obvious one, the *only* one Taramakis would have approached."

"Then what happens to your idea that the two murders were connected? Helen Zacharias, I mean?"

"It fits in perfectly," Alexander said. "Thea Malabar had only two obstacles, as far as she was concerned, to her marrying Minos Zacharias: Helen Zacharias and Ettore D'Aquilla. She killed Helen, but there was no way she could kill D'Aquilla. She was even afraid, probably with justification, to be alone with him. I mean, what if she said something that enraged him, something she thought was harmless, and he went crazy. The editorial writers would say, calmly, that killing an unfaithful wife, in America at least, is not to be condoned and that this shows we must provide legislation to get at the underlying hypocrisy of our culture. But she'd still be dead. No, Thea Malabar had to get someone else to kill her husband of record. It could not be a professional killer, obviously, and it had to be someone she controlled. Only Gregor Brezhnikov fills that bill. And, as I first said, it all stems from the murder of Helen Zacharias a year ago. Absolutely. My problem is, how do I handle Demetrios Taramakis?"

"Why do you have to handle Demetrios Taramakis? Stay away from him, Alexander. He sounds dangerous to me."

"By now, his agents in America have told him that I'm involved. If he was really behind the murder of Thea Malabar, he's not going to like my finding the killer—who knows what the killer will say when I get him?—and especially, he won't like my tying the two cases together."

"You're confusing me, Alexander. You just said that Brezhnikov killed her. Without Taramakis."

"Yes, *if* Brezhnikov killed her, it was without Taramakis. But *if* I was right about D'Aquilla . . . ? I don't want Taramakis working against me."

Working *against* Alexander? What he really meant was getting ready to *kill* Alexander, if Alexander found the murderer. I needed this? With all my troubles, I needed this too? And not just kill Alexander; what about me? And Pearl? Even Burton. What's three more, if you're rich?

If Alexander found the killer. In Alexander's mind, there was no doubt he would; of that *I* had no doubt. But maybe I could sabotage . . . ? Nah, if he ever found out—and he would—forget it. The best thing was to pray that Brezhnikov was the killer.

Please, God. *Please.*

30

"Thea Malabar," Salome Auber said in her low, sexy voice, "is one big—*une putaine, salope, assassine.*" If I understood French any better, I might have been shocked—I was pretty sure I knew what *putaine* was, and *assassine,* but *salope* they never taught in my high school—shocked to hear those words coming out of lips that even Pearl would have envied. In fact, Pearl would have envied the perfect figure, the age—Salome was ten years younger—the green eyes, everything but the short blond hair. Pearl's was better; I'll give her that.

"It seems to me, Auber"—this was for my protection; private eyes are supposed to plug sexy blondes in the belly, not treat them like china dolls—"that Thea Malabar was the victim, not a killer."

"Victim?" She laughed nastily. "Malabar? She is one big son-of-a-bitch. She make more miserable than all soprano put together in one. Ten time."

"You don't like sopranos?" Not that I cared, but if I kept her talking, sooner or later she'd tell me something useful.

"Nobody like soprano. Even other soprano. *Especial* other soprano. Worse as tenor. Much." She nodded for emphasis.

"What did Thea Malabar do to you, Auber?"

"What she do? You don't know?" Salome looked truly astonished. "Everybody know. You detective, don't know?"

"I am not *in* opera," I explained, moving slightly, so I'd interfere with Alexander's line of vision; I was more interested in his judging what she said than how she looked.

"Okay." Salome seemed mollified. She took a deep breath and I, even I, stared. "First. I am not allow to be in production with Malabar. Only the fat old. You know what this cost? Me? Money, publicity, advance career, repertoire. Everything! Two. When I am in same *season,* her name must be bigger as mine two times. Make Salome Auber look amateur. Not big star. You know what this cost? Me? Money? Three. When she is on bill, *she* get Saturday night *only*. Then she say she make full house. Ha! Even jump dog make full house Saturday night. And I must in one week three times to sing. The voice is strain, no? Make short the career, no? You know how much *this* cost? Me? Four. When . . . No. Is enough. Too much. Nobody could stand. Only Salome Auber. Like saint. Patience. Salome say nothing."

"Four." I finished it for her. "Whenever she was in the same city as you, she stole your men. Deliberately."

"It is to lie." Blondes blush easily. "I am happy marry. Malabar try to get with friends of Salome Auber because she is jealous; she have no friend. Nobody like. She know I am *most* beautiful. My friend laugh at her, ugly, old, flat, wrinkle. Very bad disposition; *nobody* can like. If I want, I could take from her. But why I want? I have nice friend. Malabar? She take anybody; ugly, dirty, *poor*. Stranger. From street. No taste, no chic."

"Was Minos Zacharias ugly, dirty, and poor?"

"Okay," she admitted, "is one. But *only* one. If I want, one smile, I can . . . But why I? Malabar jealous of *me;* I don't care who she . . . She is like dog in the street."

"Besides, on the yacht, you had Carlo Cacciare." Time to shake her up a bit.

"She say that? She lie. I tell you she is jealous. *She* want Carlo, but he don't like. He want *me,* always after me. Is amuse, but I happy marry." She laughed. It was natural, charming, perfect; must have taken lots of practice.

"When did you find out about Helen Zacharias' murder?" Another jolt for her; like shooting fish in a barrel.

"Murder? No. Accident. Why you say—? You are sure?"

"I'm a detective." I gave her my dowager duchess look. "We have just uncovered evidence that—" Let her imagination spread the fear. "So, Auber, when did you find out?"

"Next morning." She was looking at me carefully now, trying to see if I thought she was implicated in any way or, worse, would make public her fling with Carlo Cacciare. Boaster he might have been, but about Salome I was now positive. "I go to bed very early." I never doubted *that,* kiddo. "My throat, it is very delicate. The air of the sea. I am *artiste,* you understand? I see nothing, I hear nothing. Very shock when the captain tell me next day."

Alexander couldn't contain himself any longer. "Salome, you're a liar." She shook her head weakly. Alexander was acting really tough, and with his gorillalike looks, it doesn't take all that much acting. "If you lie to a detective about little things, he is likely to think you're lying about *big* things. Do you understand?"

"I? Lie? No, monsieur, I do not lie."

"All right, Salome. I'll tell you something that only Lieutenant Warshafsky and I know; we work together. One of the four TV cameras was loaded with ultraviolet sensitive film, with a strong ultraviolet spotlight shining on the set. You understand?"

"Ultraviolet? To see in the dark?"

"Clearly. Right through the scrim. Everything is on tape. Recorded. *Everything.*"

"*Mon Dieu.* But it was only acting. Maddalena was—in the opera she go up to the Duke to . . . *Acting.* For the *opera.*"

"The tape clearly shows you were not wearing panties, Salome." Pure guesswork, of course, but it was a natural. I mean, how else? "And no one in the audience could have seen a thing; it was totally dark on the second floor, so who were you and Carlo acting for?"

"Please"—she began crying—"please. My husband. My children. You must not . . . it was only—"

"You want me to destroy the tape?" She nodded wordlessly. I'm sure that if I had not been scheduled to be there, she would have saved the wear and tear on another pair of panties, just in case. Damned frugal, our Salome. And always prepared, no? "What will you do for me if I . . . not destroy, but suppress the tape?"

She shot a swift glance at me—class will always tell—and decided not to offer Alexander the supreme sacrifice or, in her case, the usual. In front of his wife, at least. "I do . . . What you want, Mr. Gold?"

"The truth." Alexander muffed his chance, thank God. Also saved himself the opportunity to get his head handed to him when we got home. "Answer all my questions with the absolute truth. The *complete* truth, understand?" She nodded, brightening, now that the immediate threat was removed. "Okay, Salome, when Gilda came into the inn and you threw the cloth over her head, you stabbed her with your left hand. Where had you hidden the knife? In your bra? Down your back?"

"No. I do not kill her. How I can kill her? I am holding her left arm with my left hand and the cloth with my right hand. Ask Brezhnikov. He will tell."

"Brezhnikov is in love with you, Salome. He'd lie for you."

"No, no. I do nothing with Brezhnikov. Only work."

"He says you encouraged him, led him on. Smiled at him."

"No. Yes, I smile all time. For everybody. Very friend. Look on Malabar arm. I hold very tight. I am strong. There will be mark. You will see."

"You were trying to hurt her arm? Under cover of the action?"

"No, no. In opera, I must hold Gilda so, for Sparafucile to kill. Must hold very tight."

"So tightly the marks would remain ten minutes later? Come on, Salome, no lying. Or else."

"Okay. I want Malabar understand she must stop make trouble for me. No more."

"Otherwise you'd kill her?"

"No. Otherwise I make trouble for *her.*"

Alexander relaxed slightly, deliberately, I thought. "That's better, Salome. Of course you didn't stab her with your left hand. The cameras show you sliding your right hand under the cloth. That's when you stabbed her."

"No, no. It is not to stab. It is accident. She move."

"She moved? With you holding tightly to her left arm and Sparafucile holding tightly to her right arm? You're lying again, Salome."

"No, no. Sparafucile is not holding Malabar."

"Not holding Malabar?" Alexander was hamming it up, but Salome was too upset to notice. "But the camera shows him with his left hand under the cloth. What was he doing, then?"

"Maybe he is stab Malabar?"

"Good! Excellent. We'll go interview Brezhnikov. I'll tell him you accused him of killing Thea Malabar. Let's see what he says about that."

"No, no!" She looked around frantically. "I don't say . . . It . . . I do not accuse—"

"You just did, Salome. Are you afraid he'll tell us about your affair?"

"No. Don't. It was not *affaire*. Real. Only little . . . flirt. Nothing." Opera seems to have all sorts of fringe benefits I never imagined. Pearl would have a jealous fit when I told her I knew about it before she did.

"So," Alexander pressed on, "if he was not stabbing Thea Malabar, you must have been doing it with your right hand. What other reason was there for your hand under the cloth?"

There was no escape for her. "It was joke. Only little joke, you see? I am put my hand on her neck, very gentle, to show I can . . . make trouble also. Brezhnikov say it is not professional to do; he hold my hand. Go ask; I don't care. Is true. I am not stab Malabar, can not stab, because Brezhnikov hold my hand."

Another good lead shot to hell. Unless the two of them were in cahoots, which was very unlikely, and were a lot smarter than Alexander, which was impossible. "So you told Brezhnikov you were going to frighten Malabar a little?"

"Yes. Little bit."

"You told him in bed."

"No, no. Only little flirt." She was regaining her composure.

"Brezhnikov says you told him in bed," Alexander said brutally, "that you were going to scratch her eyes out when Gilda screamed in the opera, and claim it was an accident." These prima donnas are not all that far from the jungle. Pearl would die twice when I told her this too. "Don't try any more lies, Salome. You don't know how much I know, and I'm losing patience with you."

"No, no. Brezhnikov speaks . . . his English is . . . He does not understand. I just want do *one* little scratch *near* the eye."

"That's it, Salome. You know that most educated Russians

speak perfect French; it's almost a second language among the cultured. And all opera singers know French, Italian, and German. You had no trouble at all communicating with Brezhnikov." In any way, *that* I would swear to. "So I'm going to turn over the ultraviolet tape of you and Cacciare to the newspapers." He got up to leave. Dutifully, I got up too, although I knew it was a waste of motion.

It was. Salome Auber deflated at once. "No, No. Sit. Please sit, I will . . ."

Alexander sat down, acting reluctant. "All right, but this is it. I knew you didn't kill Malabar when Gilda first came into the inn. You killed her later, when you stood in front of her, back to the audience, just before you went upstairs. To Cacciare."

"No. I only—"

"Talk, Salome. No more tricks."

"I . . . Yes. Talk." She licked her lips. "I bend over Malabar. She is in sack, she can do nothing. I have candle and I hold by face, by hair. Like Maddalena examine Gilda. I say, 'See, Malabar, son-of-a-bitch, how easy I can burn hair, burn face, accident. Big scar on face.' I put hand on neck. Gentle. I say, 'See, son-of-a-bitch Malabar, how easy I squeeze larynx, not to sing anymore.' I put hand by eye. I say, 'Quiet, see, Malabar, how easy I scratch eye out, make you blind. If you run away, if you do not sing Gilda Sunday, somebody else will do for me. For you, because you son-of-a-bitch. Brezhnikov do, Cacciare do, somebody who like me do, because everybody hate you.' Then I walk up stair."

"You stopped halfway up the stairs for a moment, and turned to her."

"Yes. She turn head. She say, quiet, whisper, not even Sparafucile hear, 'I am going to have you killed.' That is all. I make like I don't hear, go up stair. Quick."

It was the truth. I knew it. There are times when you just

know. So she hadn't done it; but I never really suspected her in the first place. Not that I expected everything she *had* done, what Alexander had gotten out of her, but the most I had thought she was guilty of was covering up for the killer. So now I knew that Cacciare wasn't the killer; he was busy, pinned in place upstairs, if I visualized it correctly. And Sparafucile wasn't the murderer, either. After dragging Malabar, in the sack, to the middle post, he had been sitting by the fire, waiting for Rigoletto to come back with the fee for killing the Duke.

D'Aquilla wasn't the murderer; he was never inside the inn. Valczyk wasn't the murderer, and neither was Kreuz; both of them were backstage in their penguin outfits, waiting for the big applause. No way either of them could get to Thea Malabar. The mysterious emissary from Demetrios Taramakis? If he existed at all, how would he get into the inn? The ghost of Helen Zacharias? That way lies madness.

Minos Zacharias? He was in the box next to Max Baron during the opera. Or was he? We never checked. But what's the difference? Billionaires don't do things themselves they can hire others to do. Or do they? And if they do, *how* do they?

If Alexander failed this time—*when* he failed—I'd just keep him sedated for a month, or until he could get the proper perspective on this petty little million-dollar problem. We both should live so long. Pearl and Burton too; they deserve a long life. Or instead of sedation, I'd keep him stuffed with chocolate; same thing. Or should I tell Salome Auber she had my permission, provided she didn't tell Alexander she had it; clearly she didn't care who she fooled around with for one night, and Alexander would be a new, I hope, experience for her. The sexual guilt, coupled with the ever-present basic Jewish guilt, would keep him from blaming me for messing up the case. For a week, at least. And who knows? In a week, we could maybe get a *normal* impossible case. The things I do for A.I.K.

Well, if you want to be a private eye, you have to play by the rules. And it really didn't slip my attention that, if and when— guaranteed *when,* rather than *if*—I needed to have him owe me a really big one, or even two, I could always tell him I *knew.* And that I could tell by his *eyes.* That would keep him from getting any *more* ideas. Just in case.

31

"That was another terrific interrogation, Alexander," I said. The moment called for a lifting of his spirit. "We really learned a lot." Yeah. All bad.

"It was easy, Norma; she's such a clumsy liar. Couldn't she see the inconsistencies in what she said? How damaging it was to repeat what an angel she is and how bad Malabar was? How many times did she insist she was happily married? At least twice?"

"Well, people with something to hide have to lie. Would you expect her to confess all her sins right away? And when you look like Salome Auber, you don't have to lie convincingly; you just bat your eyelashes, wiggle your *tochus,* and half the population of the world will believe you don't even go to the toilet."

"She knew better than to try that on me."

"With me present, she did. If I weren't there, you'd have gotten the full treatment." Horizontally, I'm sure. "Too bad we lost Sparafucile."

"If Salome told the truth, and I'm sure she did, all it means is that Malabar was alive at the time Salome went upstairs. But Sparafucile had another chance when he went back to drag out the sack."

"That was only a few seconds, Alexander. Not enough time."

"How much time did he need? He opens the sack wider and holds it with his right hand, pushes Malabar's head in, and at the same time stabs her—he's in perfect position for that—only a second, yanks the sack closed, and ties the cord around the neck of the sack. Easy."

"What about screaming, struggling?"

"The music would cover some sound. But the sack had to be padded; you can't drag a big star on the floor in a thin sack. That would also absorb some sound. And the struggling could never be seen while the sack is being dragged, especially down the two steps at the entrance to the inn. The bouncing around with the knife in her would cause more damage. You heard what Burton said. She'd lose consciousness in ten seconds."

"So Brezhnikov did it?" We're back in business again.

"He's the only one who could have."

"But how do we prove it?"

"I can't. That's what's bothering me right now. There's no way. At least nothing that will stand up in court."

"It doesn't have to stand up in court, darling. As long as the police charge him with the murder."

"If you were Warshafsky, Norma, would you arrest him on just what we have now?"

"Now that we know who it is, we'll get the evidence. Maybe Kreuz has something we don't know about."

"Him? He's smarter than all the rest put together. From him, we'll only get what he wants us to know."

So what else is new? At least we knew who the murderer was. But with my luck, Kreuz would tell us something that would absolutely, positively *prove* it couldn't have been Brezhnikov.

Guaranteed.

32

"**I** know why they call me 'the Nazi' behind my back, Hugo Kreuz said, "but I expected better of you, Mr. Gold."

"You did fight with the Wehrmacht," Alexander said.

"It was almost impossible to avoid, then, and I was on the Eastern Front, where they sent the ones they wanted killed. Didn't millions of Americans fight with your armies?"

"America wasn't a fascist country, Kreuz. And your father was a member of the party."

"A high percentage, Gold, of adult male Germans signed up in the early stages. It was, after all, the National *Socialist Workers Party* of Germany. Its program wasn't very different from what present-day Socialist parties propose or what Roosevelt put through in 1932. Even the Communists voted Nazi in '32. And speaking of fascism, Mussolini, who named fascism, was a Socialist too."

"Hitler documented his anti-Semitism in *Mein Kampf.*"

"My father was an anti-Semite; is that my fault? Aren't some people in America, even today? I was a baby in '28, and eight years old in '32. What would you have me do? Why not look at my record, Gold? Is there any sign of prejudice there?"

"According to the record, you act like a dictator. Prussian style. Everyone says so."

Kreuz sighed. "It's my appearance. I cannot help that I look like Erich von Stroheim, who was Jewish, by the way. Nor can I help that, to the lay public, Stroheim—who was a great artist, a great actor and director; in real life the opposite of the roles he played—to them Stroheim represented the Prussian militarist. As far as being a dictator, it is my job, my function, to make decisions. I make them quickly and firmly, with no . . . eh, no *Zögern? Schwafeln?*"

"Hesitance? Waffling?"

"Yes, no waffling; a good word. That is dictatorship? I give precise orders, so there will be no misunderstanding. It is a terrible thing for a subordinate not to know what is wanted, to know that *whatever* he does, he is wrong. Some managers do this deliberately, so they can later blame. I do not. That is *not* dictatorship. I make accurate, detailed contracts, with strong penalties for both sides. I keep my agreements and I insist others do the same. Otherwise, how to function? One cannot plan properly three years in advance without absolute dependability by all parties to the contracts. That is not dictatorship; it is proper management."

"There are articles and interviews that claim you treat singers like animals. Slaves."

"You tell me what you would do, Gold. A famous singer, with whom I have contracted two years ago to give five performances of a brand-new production for which I have spent a fortune, sends a letter—does not phone three days earlier, mind you—that she cannot attend the first week's rehearsals because Jou-Jou, her pussycat, has been out of sorts and will be upset by flying. Would I please send a chauffered Rolls for her? To Salt Lake City?"

"I would send her a letter, Kreuz, one-cent postage due, saying that I understand her terrible predicament but, unfortunately, the contract makes no provision for special transportation, and certainly not paid for by the Pantheon; that if she is not here on time I will be forced to hire another singer, one I consider better suited to the role, invoke the penalty clauses of the contract, bill her for the additional cost of the substitute—whom I will pay twice as much as the original, due to the emergency—and include a copy of the press release, illustrated by some very unflattering photos, describing her physical infirmities, due to age, naturally, and her unfeeling lack of responsibility to her *ex*-fans, which will appear in next Sunday's *Times*."

"Not bad for an amateur, Gold, but you forgot to add that the singer I substitute will be the one Jou-Jou's mother hates the most. Now, what if you get a telegram from a singer who claims to be deathly ill, dying almost, which says she must miss an important performance. Your spies tell you she has decided to stay in Mississippi an extra day because her new local boyfriend has persuaded her to appear at the opening of his three new shopping centers at a thousand dollars per appearance, and she will sing a country-western song at each."

"I send the company physician down to examine her, a full examination, including a proctoscopy, a Pap smear, a six-hour glucose-tolerance test, and a full gastrointestinal series. In the barium mixture he puts a powerful laxative. He then holds a press conference and describes, in highly exaggerated detail, everything he checked and any minor anomalies he found in her anatomy. He concludes by saying that he doubts if she will ever sing again, given her infirmities and advanced age, made worse by dissipation, but if she does sing, her voice will never be the same. I would also take sound movies of each shopping center opening and exhibit them in the lobby of the Pantheon before the performance of that opera. What did you do, Kreuz?"

"About the same, but no laxative. My doctor did not have the proper attitude, and I had to hold the press conference myself. How would you like to be my deputy, Gold? I retire in three years."

"I don't like opera all that much, Kreuz."

"That's too bad. To stay on this job, you must love opera more than life. It is all right to hate singers, though. Mandatory, in fact."

"Do you really hate them all, Kreuz?"

"Not so much as when I was younger. I was more intense, then. Every production had to be perfect; everything had to be right. Today, I am a little more tolerant of stupidity, although I cannot stand incompetence, or lack of cooperation, in a professional. And I absolutely will not stand for deliberate sabotage for personal gain, although . . . Fortunately, the animals have learned well from my early lessons. Very few challenge me now; they know I will retaliate ten times over. And my life is made beautiful quite often these days by the truly professional ladies and gentlemen who are now performing, who are now the great majority. The younger ones, the beautiful girls and boys— it is so sweet. They love music, they understand music, they are always prepared, always listen to the director, always good-willed. Not like some others I have known in the past. Our goal is to have a balanced repertory company. Of course, there will always be stars, and deservedly so, but they will be less important than they are now."

"You've never worked outside of Europe before, have you?"

"You have prepared a dossier on me, I see. Yes, I have a problem with ships, and do not much care for flying either. Since I have been in the United States, I have not gone back, and will not go until I retire. I did work at the Edinburgh Festival one season; it was there I was fortunate enough to meet Helen Zacharias. A remarkable woman who . . . a great patron of the arts and a gifted musician in her own right. Her death was a great loss to the world of music. And to me, personally."

"You were close to her? Friends?"

"Very close, professionally. And I was very grateful to her. She was instrumental . . . From Edinburgh, she induced me to go with her to a production of *Il Ré Pastore* at Glyndebourne. A minor piece, but done so cleverly, so perfectly, that I insisted on meeting the director. It was then she introduced me to Jan Valczyk. We hit it off so well—it was as though a missing piece of me had been suddenly fitted in—that I broached an idea I had been thinking of for a year: To have a summer festival of operas with Greek themes, played in an amphitheater near Athens, using Greek singers. *Alceste, Médee, Oedipus Rex, Elektra,* and, of course, *La Belle Hélène.* Valczyk loved the idea, and that very night we planned the basic arrangements. Helen Zacharias underwrote it, and with the help of her friends and the Greek government, we put it on only one year later. It was a great artistic success, and almost broke even financially. This was the turning point in my career, and Valczyk's too. Two years later, the Pantheon sought me out, and here I am."

"So when Thea Malabar killed Helen Zacharias, you swore to make her suffer for it."

"Of course. I did, and so, I am sure, did the many others who loved Helen Zacharias. I could not prove it, but I knew in my heart what had happened. I also felt some responsibility for the matter, since I had suggested the gathering on Helen's yacht to her. She loved the idea, unfortunately for all of us."

"You knew Thea Malabar before? What was she like?"

"Very well," Kreuz said bitterly.

"What did Thea Malabar do to you personally, Kreuz?"

"It was long ago. I had just been named general manager of a good-sized opera company in Germany; my first really big chance. Malabar had just become famous. She was the mistress—this was before Minos Zacharias, though I am sure it would have made little difference to her if it had been after—the mistress of the chairman of the board of the opera company. My contract had not yet been signed, although everything had been agreed. She insisted I fire the director and the conductor. Why? They did not cooperate. The conductor would not transpose her music a tone—a full tone—down so she could take the high notes without strain. The most he would do was a half tone and hope that some critic with perfect pitch would not catch it. And the director would not light her more than everybody else, or let her upstage anybody, or let her stand up for the death scene. My contract was not signed. I had to resign, of course. It set back my timetable, my career, five years. I should have been at the Pantheon or the Met ten years ago. It almost killed my wife. We had to defer having another child and, when I was back on the track again, I was in my mid-forties and my wife in her late thirties. The time was past. You want a motive, Mr. Gold? For killing Thea Malabar? There it is."

"Rigoletto?" How Alexander makes these leaps of reasoning, intuition, is still beyond me. "The one she got you fired from?"

"Of course, *Rigoletto.* Isn't it obvious, Gold? *Rigoletto* is not quite the greatest role for a soprano; it is a baritone's opera, the greatest there is for a baritone, and I gave the title role to the man she hated and feared the most, her husband, Ettore D'Aquilla."

"So this performance was your revenge on her?"

"Precisely. Although I did not intend for her to be killed. But I would not have minded a bit if D'Aquilla—she was sure to do something to irritate him; it was her nature—if D'Aquilla lost his temper and strangled her onstage. We would have sold out for the rest of the season."

"You arranged everything to go wrong for her?"

"Only that which I controlled myself. I cannot control stars or directors, nor would I like to work with puppets and zombies. All I did was to bring together the proper elements. I was sure they would do the rest. And they did."

"How did you get her to work with the cast you selected? I understood she could keep out anyone she pleased."

"In a practical sense, yes, but not legally. It would have been easy for a star of her caliber to get laryngitis just before a performance, or to pull her back if she didn't like someone in the cast. To placate her, we would have to substitute some other singer. Actually, it never came to that. The threat would be sufficient, so that most managers would check with her before announcing the cast. But this is something we would never put into the contract; it would be abdicating my responsibility, my function, completely."

"So you chose the cast that would give her the most pain?"

"Exactly. D'Aquilla, of course, was the centerpiece. She really feared him; he had a terrible temper. A great artist, and a true professional, very easy to work with, his word was his bond, but if you cheated him, or fooled him, beware. I was pleased to note that Malabar made very sure never to be alone with him."

"And Kerfiu? How did he fit in?"

"He was also a great voice, a great musician. I put together the best possible cast, I assure you. I wanted this to be the greatest *Rigoletto* of all time. But his idea of acting was realism. If he had to grab you roughly, you had bruises on your arms for a week. He was almost as big as Brezhnikov, and even stronger. But, even more important, he was suffering from prostate cancer, and a series of operations and the allied treatment, all unpublicized, of course, had left him sexually nonfunctional. The strain may even have contributed to his untimely death."

"So this removed another potential ally or confidant from

Malabar's power, leaving her isolated in the cast. But what about Cacciare? Didn't he already—with Malabar—weren't *they* close?"

"Cacciare was never close with anybody, except physically, and Malabar was too forceful, not the type of woman he really liked. But to make sure, I brought in Salome Auber. She and Cacciare, they're two of a kind. With her around, Cacciare would spit on Malabar. And, best of all, Salome hated Malabar, and made no bones about it. But you must realize, too, that I did not compromise on the quality of the voices."

"And Jan Valczyk? Did he hate Malabar too?"

"He didn't know her, except for that week on the yacht; he'd never worked with her before. But that didn't matter; his normal way of working was to treat the singers like robots. Respectfully, yes, helpfully, but they had to do everything *exactly* his way. He was very firm, uncompromising. I knew this would drive Malabar crazy, and it did. She complained to me twice a day. I was regretful, but with me, the director directs, not the performer."

"Why did she stand for this? Why didn't she just walk away?"

"You tell me, Gold; you may yet end up deputy director of the Pantheon."

"That's easy. You paid her a higher-than-usual fee, even for her, and contracted with her first. When she found out who her colleagues were to be and threatened to walk out, you read her the penalty clause in your contract with the Tay-Sachs Benefit Committee and told her what it would cost her to mess around. Right?"

"Which clause I *encouraged* Mr. Hanslik to put in, even though he may not remember it that way. And I put into each singer's contract—it looked harmless at the time—that each would be bound by the base contract with the Benefit Committee, and guaranteed to give a full performance. Thea Malabar was very respectful of money; greedy, actually. Considering her origins, it was understandable, but . . . I also told her that if she walked out, I would announce that, given her *true* age, she felt that her voice had been roughening somewhat, of late, and she felt she would be unable to give a performance equal to that of her distinguished colleagues, and especially, her husband. Further, I would let it be known that Malabar hated benefits and benefit audiences, and since Tay-Sachs Disease affected only Jews, she saw no need to waste her waning talents on such an insignificant group."

"You really *flayed* her."

"That's not all; I contrived a few tricks of my own. Her costumes, which fitted perfectly in the dress rehearsals, had the seams taken in a full inch just before the performance, and the excess material was cut off, so it was impossible to let them out again. It not only made her look as though she had gained weight, it restricted her breathing somewhat, so that she had to gasp for breath onstage, which made her look like an amateur with emphysema. And I told Valczyk to keep her head in the sack after Gilda was killed."

"But it didn't happen that way," Alexander said.

"No, I'm sorry to say. He felt it would be more dramatic to keep her head visible while Rigoletto was paying off Sparafucile for killing the Duke. He was right, of course. But I asked him to light her more brightly, and he agreed, so that she had to hold her head down and couldn't move for ten minutes before she sang the dying duet with Rigoletto. And having to play almost dead, and being in a sack, she couldn't stretch or draw a full breath, which would have made her singing come off a poor second to Rigoletto's."

"That didn't come off, thanks to the killer."

"No, but didn't that finale work well? I would be tempted to do all future *Rigoletto*s that way—I don't mean kill the sopranos, of course, though the thought is tempting—were it not for my great respect for Verdi."

"You really ruined her top notes in the 'Caro Nome' with that tight dress. Is that showing respect for Verdi?"

"You noticed, eh?" Kreuz smiled like a wolf. "That made the revenge, the vendetta, complete; fully rounded. You know, *Rigoletto* is sometimes called *La Maledizione*—'The Curse.' When Malabar got me fired from that first *Rigoletto,* I swore revenge, a curse on her, just as Monterone did on Rigoletto in the opera. It wasn't just the costume that made her sing so badly, and it was really all her fault."

"She caused her own doom?"

"In a way, yes, and I was so taken with the idea that I compromised my respect for the music, for producing a perfect opera. She *insisted,* as part of the deal, that Edelstein transpose her big solo one-and-one-half tones down from what Verdi had written. All through rehearsals, down through final dress rehearsal, we did it that way. Then, for the performance—I had intended to *raise* it a half tone *above* the proper key. Edelstein loved the idea, even though it meant a lot of extra work for him and for the orchestra, especially for the flute soloist. But I couldn't bring myself to spoil the opera, and neither could Edelstein, so he played 'Caro Nome' in its proper key. Malabar had to sing her big solo a full tone-and-a-half above what she had prepared for. She screeched like a crow on the top notes and she knew it and she knew I knew it. It was delicious. Did you read the critics?"

"No," Alexander said, "but I'd hate to have you for an enemy. Did Edelstein hate her too?"

Kreuz nodded. "He did something on his own I should have thought of. Usually, when it's dark in a theater, the conductor uses a lighted baton, so the musicians and singers can pick up the beat easily. Valczyk didn't want a light dancing around in the orchestra—it would have spoiled the effect—so Edelstein used a white-enameled baton. There was enough glow from the stage so it could be seen against his dark clothes. But when Malabar sang, he held it right in front of his shirt front, white on white, and made very small movements. Malabar went crazy trying to see it."

"You didn't pull any punches, did you?"

"I had been waiting for the opportunity for years. I shouldn't speak ill of the dead, but she was really a terrible person."

"The yacht trip? Another part of your revenge?"

"Of course. Helen Zacharias offered the treat—it was a period when we were all vacationing—but I couldn't go, of course. Helen said her husband—who did not like me, for some reason; probably Malabar told him some lies—would be gone for most of the trip, but even if I could have brought myself to go, my presence would have been harmful to the plan. But it all worked out as I had hoped, except for Helen, obviously. Salome and Carlo recognized each other for what they were immediately, so Malabar didn't have a chance with him. Kerfiu, of course, had no interest in any woman at that time, and didn't particularly like Malabar anyway. Valczyk, of course, never became intimate, or even friendly, with performers. Minos Zacharias was away from the first day of the trip, so Malabar was left all alone, without a man, which was, for her, a great tragedy, made worse because it was in full view of Helen Zacharias. Helen, of course, from what I heard, was *very* sympathetic with Malabar's plight. Overly sympathetic, if you know what I mean. It could not have been better."

"Couldn't Thea have amused herself with the captain? Or some of the other crew members?" Alexander knew the answer, but was fishing.

"On Minos Zacharias' own ship? With his own employees?

For Minos, such a loss of face could not be tolerated. A veritable Greek tragedy. Zacharias would have killed Malabar along with the captain, publicly. For business reasons, if for nothing else."

"It seems to me, Kreuz, that you are taking for granted that Thea Malabar killed Helen Zacharias."

"Of course she did. Who else would? Or want to? Helen was loved by everybody."

"Didn't Minos Zacharias want to marry Thea Malabar?"

"I'm sure the thought crossed his mind now and then. In bed. But by daylight? Never. Not only was Helen a great help to him in business—he left her in charge, in Greece, for days at a time when he traveled—but I'm sure he genuinely liked her."

"Then why did he accept the verdict of accidental death?"

"What would you have him do? Try to bribe the investigating magistrate? Possibly he decided to handle the problem in his own way. You may not know this, but he was about to marry Patricia Horgan, not Thea Malabar. Maybe the idea of marrying his wife's murderer was more than even he could stomach."

"So you believe Minos Zacharias killed Thea Malabar?"

"Not with his own hands, Mr. Gold, but who else?"

"How?"

"Ah, Mr. Gold, if you don't know that, who would? And if you do find out, Mr. Gold, will you accuse your own client?" Hugo Kreuz smiled knowingly.

33

"**I** notice you didn't ask him if he killed Thea Malabar," I said to Alexander, "or ask him where he was at the time of the murder."

"I know where he was, Norma. Backstage, stage right, near the light traps. And I didn't need to hear him say he was innocent. What else would he say?"

"You asked everybody else; why not him?"

"Just to get their reaction. With him, nothing would show. I wanted to let him talk. You notice he gave me tons of information I didn't ask for?"

"Yep. All designed to show he was guilty of the minor crime of hating Thea Malabar, but could not have killed her."

"Of course. Burying me under a mountain of detail, all of which, I am sure, is true. What I want to know is what he left out."

"We can go over my recorder tapes tonight after supper to see if we missed anything important. Or would you rather see *Rigoletto* again tonight? With Anna Whatshername tap-tapping her dainty way across Rigoletto's garden?"

He didn't even smile. "I have the videotape engraved on my

brain. If I want to check anything I can always look at that again. Besides, you'd never get a ticket for tonight. The mobs will be out; maybe there'll be another murder, they hope."

"They'll be wasting their money, Alexander. This was no mad killer of Gildas; he had Thea Malabar ticketed from the start."

"From before that. Thea Malabar was doomed the night she killed Helen Zacharias."

"Oh, come on, Alexander. For that to be the case, Kreuz and Valczyk had to be accomplices too. You don't think this whole production was designed for the sole purpose of killing Thea Malabar, do you? I mean, there are cheaper ways, by far."

"Of course not." He was particularly irritable today, and I could understand why. "The murderer took advantage of the production to make his plans. You don't think that *nobody* besides Valczyk and Kreuz knew what it would be like a year ago, do you? How long does it take to prepare the special candles and the brackets with the compressed air hoses? The air compressors and the storage tanks? The control consoles? *Especially* the control consoles? And the set design and construction? The costumes? Lots of people knew about this production, and worked on it for a year. Even the stagehands, who had to put the sets into place and break them down. Anyone who *really* wanted to know what was going on, and was willing to take the trouble, could have found out. And even then, do you think there weren't changes made up to the last rehearsal? Which reminds me, call Kreuz later and tell him not to touch the last-scene set after tonight's performance."

"They wouldn't anyway; tomorrow's Monday, no performance. What do you have in mind, a reenactment?" This didn't bother me, since it wouldn't be coming out of our pocket.

"You never know." He sounded mysterious.

I couldn't believe this. "You know who did it already?"

"How *could* I know?" he snapped. "We just finished talking to Kreuz a few minutes ago. I haven't even had time to listen to your tapes. Stop hounding me." I was wrong. He not only didn't know; he didn't have the *slightest* idea, or even an approach. When he has a puzzle figured out, he gets very expansive, confident, excited.

"I told Pearl to make chocolate mousse for desert tonight." Better an extra pound than an ulcer. Yesterday I knew already that today would be a tough one.

"Real chocolate mousse? Not with gelatine?" He was really in a *mood* today.

"Real. With whipped cream."

"Real whipped cream?" *So* suspicious.

"I told her real whipped cream. With vanilla sugar." I hadn't—*two* pounds on him I didn't need—but as soon as I got to a phone, I would. This was no time for halfway measures.

"A full portion?" He should be so thorough questioning Kreuz, not his own loyal, honest wife of twenty-eight years.

"Absolutely," I said, making a mental note to tell Pearl the *normal* size cups too.

He was silent for a moment, then, "What do you think, Norma?" Bad. *Really* bad. He had never asked my opinion on any kind of a puzzle before. We'd better have garlic bread tonight too.

"I think you should forget about Helen Zacharias and concentrate on two things: Who actually killed Thea Malabar, and how to convict Minos Zacharias."

"You believe Hugo Kreuz?"

"It's not a question of belief. What Kreuz said was logical, but that doesn't mean he didn't do it himself. Or that Minos Zacharias didn't put him up to it."

His face was down. "You may be right, Norma, but answer

this first: How does a man in formal clothes cross a stage, even one that's not well lit, thirty feet of stage, in full view of two thousand people and four cameras, kill a woman, and then cross back, without being seen?"

Me? Alexander asking *me?* I'd have to tell Pearl to make enough mousse for seconds. And not just for Alexander either.

34

"**A**re you telling me"—Burton looked dumbfounded—
"that you can prove *none* of them did it?" Pearl had
had the good sense to make a triple recipe of the chocolate
mousse; Alexander was so drugged with chocolate, he didn't
raise his voice even a little.

"Not quite *prove*, Burt," he said. "But if you believe what
they said, and I do—and Norma does too, right, Norma?" I
nodded agreement—"if what they're saying is true, none of
them could have killed Thea Malabar."

"But the way you described it during supper," Burton said,
"Sparafucile could easily have killed Gilda when he pushed her
head into the sack and tied the cord."

"I thought so, at first," Alexander said, "but then I realized
that if Maddalena could hear Malabar's last words, so could
Sparafucile. Brezhnikov was sitting next to the fireplace, no further from Malabar than Salome Auber was."

"That doesn't mean he couldn't have done it." Burton still
didn't see the point.

"It means he *wouldn't* have done it, Burt. Once he realized
that Salome Auber knew Malabar was alive at that time, the

only one who touched Malabar, who could have killed Malabar, was Gregor Brezhnikov. Under those conditions, only a moron would have gone through with the murder. Assuming, that is, that Brezhnikov intended to kill her in the first place."

"Maybe he figured that we would think that way," Pearl said, "and went ahead and did it anyway, because he knew we would be sure he didn't. Russians are all chess players, you know, even the singers."

"Would you risk your life on that subtlety, Pearl?" I asked. "And what if we were one degree smarter and figured that *he* would figure that way, and therefore he was positively guilty? And don't forget the police, who know from nothing about subtlety. By them, if he's the only one who could have done it, he did it. Period."

"What if Salome Auber and Brezhnikov were in cahoots?" Pearl asked.

"If they were," I said, "why did she admit Malabar said anything? She could just have left it that *she* threatened Malabar."

"Salome said it to prove she was innocent."

"Not quite innocent, Pearl," Alexander said. "Just not guilty of murder. But then, when Brezhnikov finds out she betrayed him, he could say Salome was the murderer and he noticed Malabar was dead when he stuffed her into the sack. No, Pearl, no way *any* of them worked together. Too risky."

"I just thought of something," I said. "Morgan. Captain Morgan. He could be covering up for Kreuz. We only have Morgan's word that the floor of the inn was solid, no trapdoors."

"It's solid, all right," Burton said. "That was one of the first things Warshafsky checked. Besides, there's no way anyone could have crawled around down there without getting his tails all wrinkled. And his white shirt all messed up."

"How about a coverall?" I said. "For the trapeze, or whatever the killer used, he could have slipped on a coverall. Like the fancy jumpsuit Valczyk wore when we met him."

"No good," Alexander said. "The four singers were in costume; no way for any of them to get a coverall, much less put it on. And if Kreuz or Valczyk appeared in a coverall, someone would have noticed. It wasn't all that dark backstage."

"Cacciare could have stashed a coverall in the upstairs room before the performance started," I said.

"Over a Duke's costume?" Alexander sounded skeptical. "How did he get downstairs? And over to Malabar? And upstairs again? For this he'd have to have the cooperation of Salome Auber. Completely out of the question."

"He could have killed Malabar *before* Salome went upstairs," I said. "While she was putting out the candles."

"When it was ten times as light as later, after the candles were out?" Alexander said. "Then why did Salome say Malabar spoke to her?"

"Ventriloquism?" I asked. "Maybe Salome just *thought* Malabar spoke to her. Maybe it was—who else?—the killer?"

"The only one around at that time was Brezhnikov," Alexander said. "I don't think he'd make a very good ventriloquist in English. Or even Russian."

"All right," I said. "Every suggestion I make, you knock down. So who did it, Alexander? A stranger? A stagehand? Who?"

"Minos Zacharias. He knew Malabar had killed his wife. Either he couldn't bring himself to marry his wife's murderer, or he was afraid that if he did marry Thea, Demetrios Taramakis would take this as proof that Zacharias and Malabar had conspired to kill Helen."

"So why kill Thea Malabar? Just so he could marry Patricia Horgan? He didn't have to kill anyone to do that."

"The reason he gave us for marrying Patricia Horgan was

probably true, at least partly. But he also had to have considered that this marriage would prove to Demo Taramakis that Zacharias had nothing to do with Helen's death. But what must have happened, when Malabar found out about the coming marriage, she threatened Zacharias that she would tell Taramakis that it was Zacharias who had asked her to kill Helen, that she had refused, and that Zacharias must have bribed one of the sailors to do it."

"You're sure, then," I asked, "that Minos Zacharias killed Thea Malabar? Absolutely sure?"

"Not *absolutely* sure," he said, looking troubled. "If Zacharias did it, ordered it, it could only have been one of those six, most likely one of the singers. But how? Granted, Zacharias is smart enough to figure out the technique, or more likely, the misdirection. Would he depend on a singer to pull it off? Whatever was done, it had to have *some* measure of complexity, especially of timing. Opera singers are *working* on stage. They not only have to remember lines and blocking, they have to be alert for musical cues. Opera audiences are very unforgiving of blunders. If you were Minos Zacharias, would you trust an opera singer to do something like this during a performance? And worse, what if the singer made a mistake? Could Zacharias' emissary be traced back to Zacharias? Wouldn't it be easier for Zacharias to get someone to push Malabar under a truck? It just doesn't figure."

"Kreuz worked very hard," I reminded him, "to make his revenge tie in with *Rigoletto*. The opera, I mean. Couldn't that be why she was killed *during* the opera?"

"Sure it could. There are lots of 'coulds.' But what happened? What *really* happened?"

There was dead silence, Alexander was staring into space. It was time to call a halt. I gave Pearl the nod; she and Burton went home.

I took Alexander's hand. "Let's go to bed early, darling," I suggested. "Now. We've had a hard two days. Put the problem into your subconscious for a while."

"There's something one of them said to me," Alexander said. "I feel it. Something important. I wish I knew—"

"You've gone through my tapes twice tonight, darling. With me. Even if it *is* there, tired as you are, you won't find it tonight. Come to bed. I'll listen again with you tomorrow."

He went reluctantly. I had the feeling that I had just bought a few hours, that tomorrow would be worse. Just before he dropped off, he whispered, "Did you call Kreuz? Tell him to leave the set in place? Just in case?"

"Yes, darling," I said. Wishful thinking, Alexander; sympathetic magic. Well, if logic and reason don't work, who am I to sneer at magic?

35

"**G**et dressed," Alexander said, when I came downstairs. "I had to promise Burt buttermilk pancakes to get him to come over this early."

"No problem," I said, "but why did you get up so early? I wanted you to have a good night's sleep."

"I got enough," he said. "I just have to make some phone calls. After breakfast."

"You have an idea, Alexander? You want me to research something for you, or do you have to browse through a library yourself?"

"Not necessary. The calls are just for verification."

It was early, so I was still slow. "You know who already?"

"And how too. Everything. It was obvious."

"I just hate when you say that, Alexander. If it's so obvious, why wasn't it obvious last night when you were breaking your head over it?"

"Because I was looking for the wrong thing. It wasn't what someone said to me; it was what I said to someone. That's why I missed it."

"Alexander, if you're trying to drive me crazy—"

"No, really. Get dressed and make breakfast, and I'll tell everybody what I want you to do."

Alexander wouldn't talk and Burton wouldn't talk and Burton wouldn't listen until all the pancake batter was used up. What most people don't know is that you have to add sour cream and a little sugar to the buttermilk to get the right bite, and to make the batter thin, so the pancakes are slightly lacy. The syrup has to be homemade blueberry jam thinned with blackberry brandy. You can throw in a little kirsch too, if you're in the mood. Someday I'm going to write a cookbook. Not just recipes, but how to *create*. By me, cooking is an art form. Like opera, only healthier. Ask Thea Malabar.

"Call Demetrios Taramakis?" Burton sounded astounded. "I'll never get through to him."

"Don't you know anyone who knows him?" Alexander asked. "Max Baron, maybe?"

"Minos Zacharias knows him," Burton said.

"Very funny, Burt. He's the one man I can't ask."

"I'm friendly with Norman Jakobs, of Baker & McKenzie's New York office. They're the world's biggest attorneys, offices all over the world. If they don't have an office in Athens, guaranteed they have a correspondent there."

"Good," Alexander said. "Start writing. I want this done exactly the way I say it: Demetrios Taramakis is to put one million dollars net into an escrow account with your friend Jakobs for a period of twenty-four hours, starting at five P.M. today, New York time. The money is to be transferred to A.I.K., Inc., if, within that twenty-four-hour period, Alexander Magnus Gold phones to Demetrios Taramakis at—get the number he'll be waiting at, Burt—with the name of the murderer of Helen Taramakis Zacharias, along with sufficient information to convince Demetrios Taramakis of the accuracy of this accusation. Demetrios Taramakis is to be the sole judge as to the validity of Gold's accusation and the confirming information."

"This is crazy, Alexander," I said. "Suppose he isn't at the phone when you call."

"He'll be *hanging* on the phone," Alexander said. "He'll stay awake all night if he has to. Wouldn't you, in his position?"

"All he's got to say, Alex," Burton said, "is that he doesn't believe you, and he saves a million dollars."

"He won't lie," Alexander said. "Not in a matter of personal honor. Taramakis would *want* it known that he believes, so that when the murderer disappears, everyone will know that Helen's death was properly avenged."

"Wait a minute, Alexander," I said. "This is beginning to sound like you don't have any proof. Zero."

"How *could* I have proof? It happened a year ago, five thousand miles from here."

"And you expect to convince him by phone?"

"Oh, sure. I'm one hundred percent right. No doubt about it."

I didn't like the sound of that, but what could we lose? A few phone calls to Athens and an hour's lawyers' fees? Not worth fighting about. I motioned Pearl to clean off the table.

"Something else, Burton," Alexander said. "Not that I really need it, but just for verification. When you've made the arrangements with your friend Jakobs, the international lawyer, tell him I want to talk to him before he calls Taramakis, to get some information for me from Taramakis."

"*From* Taramakis?" Burton looked at Alexander as though he, Alexander, had gone completely crazy. "You're asking a million from Taramakis for information *you're* going to give *him,* which you admit you can't prove, and you want him to get some information *for* you?"

"Just verification, Burt; I know what it *has* to be. But I'd prefer to have Taramakis check it for me; it would take me too long to do myself. He'll do it, don't worry."

"All right, Alex," Burton said, getting up, "I'll arrange it with Jakobs. But don't be surprised if Taramakis tells you to go play in traffic."

"And as soon as Jakobs has the information from Taramakis, he's to call me, okay? Good. Don't go yet; we have to make arrangements for the Malabar case."

"You did that one too?" Pearl's eyes popped.

"Didn't I always say the two were connected?" Alexander gloated. "I was absolutely right. Now here's what I want you to do."

"Hold it," I said. "You're going too fast, Alexander; trying to slip something past me. If the two cases are connected, and if you have no proof, no evidence at all for the first case, do you also have nothing for the second case?"

"Not really," he admitted, "no. The nature of the crime is such that there *can't* be any evidence in the usual sense of the word."

"No evidence? There *can't* be any evidence?" Now he'd really gone off the deep end. "What are you going to do with the killer? Suggest psychotherapy?"

"I don't need evidence," he weaseled. "When I reenact the crime, it will be obvious who the killer is."

"Be *obvious?* Then what? Our contract calls for the *arrest* of the killer, remember? Otherwise, no million dollars."

"And maybe a suit for false arrest," Burton added, "or defamation of character."

"If the police close their books on the case, we collect. I don't see how they *cannot* close their books after I reenact the crime. I'm not going to *say* anything, just do the reenactment, so there'll be no defamation."

"*You're* not going to say anything?" Burton looked very doubtful.

"No, and I don't want anyone else to say anything either."

"Hold on," I said. "Are you setting yourself up as a target, Alexander? Because if you are—"

"I'm not, Norma. Really I'm not. All I'm doing is demonstrating *how* the murder was done."

"Does the killer know that, Alexander? If he thinks you know who he is, he's going to try to kill you."

"I'm really not trying to . . . All right." He gave in. "Pearl, Burton, you can spread the word that I'm going to demonstrate how the murder was done, but emphasize that I don't know who did it." He glanced at me. "And make sure that they all understand that I haven't told Norma, or anyone else either, anything. Not the method, not my suspicions, nothing. Or told you or Pearl, especially."

"Are you really just going to reenact the crime, Alexander?" I asked. "Do you really have *no* proof?"

He squirmed. "It's not possible to have proof, Norma. Not real proof. But after I demonstrate—"

"And the killer walks?" I said. I couldn't believe this. "That's a way to solve a crime? Even Agatha Christie wouldn't let a—"

"I don't care," he shouted, because he was ashamed. "That's all I can do. There are no clues. There are no witnesses. There is no evidence. There's no way to convict, or even indict . . . What I've planned . . . Forget it," he huffed. "I'll do it all myself. As usual."

"All right, Alexander," I said. "Relax. I'll help. We'll all help, right, Burton? Pearl?"

"I'll be Gilda," she said eagerly. "I'd love to—"

"No," Burton said flatly. "The last time—"

"There is *absolutely* no danger," Alexander said. "Not the *slightest* chance. I guarantee it. It's only a reenactment to show how . . . But Anna, the cover for Gilda, will have to play the part. It's her role and she knows what to do. Sorry, Pearl, but you can come along and watch. Meanwhile, call Kreuz and tell him to have everyone there. Full costume, full set, lighting, everything but the orchestra; we'll use the audiotape."

"What about the TV cameras?" I asked.

"Definitely. We must have them. All four."

"What time?"

"Five o'clock. That should give us plenty of time."

"Make it later, Alex," Burton asked. "Overseas contracts in a foreign language don't get done quickly."

"All right, make it eight. The show starts at eight, sharp. Backstage I want everything exactly the way it was during the performance. Everybody, stagehands, stage manager, console operators, the works. And they must do everything the same as they did before, on that night."

"Kreuz and Valczyk?" I asked.

"Of course," he said. "Everything must be identical."

"Does that mean white tie and tails? Evening gowns?"

"The same ones, if possible; no changes. All of us."

"What about an audience?" Pearl asked. "Can I bring the Barons?"

"Sure, the more the merrier. Warshafsky *must* come, make sure of that."

"Extra cops?" I asked.

"That won't be necessary. I keep telling you that . . . All right, one or two. But tell Warshafsky to station them in the back of the balcony. And they are not to move unless he tells them to."

"What about Minos Zacharias?" Pearl asked. "Can he come?"

"Sure." Alexander was expansive. I could tell he wanted a big audience for his show. "Why not? His whole set of guests too."

"I have an idea," Pearl said. "Why don't we invite the *whole* audience back again? We'll rent the theater for . . ." She turned back to Alexander. "You're just going to do the last act, right?"

"Just the last *part* of the last act," he said. "From when Salome is halfway up the stairs to . . . to the finale."

"And there'll be no singing?"

"Just the tape of the performance, for timing. The singers will fake the singing."

"Great." Pearl's face glowed. "We'll get the theater dirt cheap. They're usually closed on a Monday, anyway, and we'll charge *two thousand dollars* a ticket. Everybody will want to be there, to see how it was done. Don't say anything to *anyone* until I arrange the deal with Kreuz. Tay-Sachs will get *rich*. I'll call Julia Baron and explain everything. We'll have the phone brigade operating in one hour. Everyone who was there during the murder will just *have* to be there at the denunciation."

"Sure," Alexander said. "Good idea. The more witnesses the better. But everybody must be in *exactly* the same place they were on that night."

"Not everybody who was there," I said, "will pay two thousand a ticket for a ten-minute show."

"Sure they will," Pearl gushed. "They're all rich, and it will be the social event of the year. What else is there to do on a Monday night? They'll love it; a *real* mystery solved."

"Won't they all be watching Thea Malabar?" I asked. "I mean, Anna Whatshername?"

"All the better," Alexander said. "Now all you have to do, Norma, is get me some lights."

"What kind of lights?"

"I need two big, powerful lights, like photographer's lights, very bright. You can probably rent them. With a switch, so you can snap them both on at once."

"Where do I put them?"

"On the outside wall of the inn, on the post opposite the one where Gilda is in the sack. No, make that one post toward stage right from Gilda, shining toward the back wall of the inn."

"What do I plug them into?" I asked, politely.

"Plug? Oh. Yes. I forgot. Plug them into any outlet backstage."

"You want wires all over the floor of the inn? And if I bring in anything like that, the stagehands will kill me first and then go on strike. So will the electricians."

"How about battery-operated lights?"

"A flashlight in each hand and one in my teeth? While I'm wearing my evening gown?"

"Well, then, maybe—"

"Forget it," I said. "I just figured out how to do it." I could be mysterious too. "But it's going to take me all day to set it up, so don't give me anything else to do. Okay. Now that I've got the lights set up, what do I do with them?"

"During the performance, when I say 'Lights,' you turn them both on at the same time."

"And where am I during the performance?"

"Next to the lights, of course. Where else?"

"Won't the audience see me through the scrim?"

"Not a chance. The light from the candle and its spot will be shining toward Thea Malabar."

"And the fireplace?"

"That's over thirty feet away, and it's a dull glow."

"Salome Auber will be looking in my direction when she's on the stair."

"The light of the candle she's carrying will be in her eyes. Stop worrying, I've got it all figured out. Just make sure you don't snap the lights on until I give the signal."

"Yes, master. Anything else?"

"I have to make a phone call, that's all."

"To a library? I have connections—"

"No. To an artist's representative. To verify a date, that's all.

Then I'm going to rest. And tonight, you have to help me with my tie. I always have trouble with ties."

Gladly. But it sounded too easy. And I know from bitter experience that with Alexander, *nothing* is too easy. Or even just *plain* easy. Or if it was easy *once,* it isn't anymore. If Alexander is involved, it's hard. And complicated. And bad for the nerves. My nerves.

36

It was amazing. With all the complications entailed in putting on an opera, the only hitch was that Anna Whatshername absolutely refused to play Gilda. Without even knowing the history of Alexander's guarantees, she decided to not even *act* like a coloratura who is going to be killed in real life after being killed in the opera. So Pearl got her wish. I must say, she looked a lot more like a sixteen-year-old virgin than Thea Malabar did. She blushed when I told her how beautiful she looked as Gilda, even disguised as a boy. I don't know what came over me; I just hope it wasn't a bad omen; like when you visit someone in the hospital and tell him how great he looks.

When Burton found out about Pearl, he insisted on being backstage. After absolutely positively guaranteeing that nothing, but nothing, and nobody, not even a mouse, could possibly hurt Pearl, or even come *near* her, Alexander made Burton promise not to talk to anyone, not to interfere, no matter what, and to stay in a corner, out of sight.

I was not exactly comfortable either. Pearl had to be fitted— even though I'm sure Anna Whatshername's costume did not have to be taken in at the bust for Pearl, still it took time—and made up and coiffed. So with my having to sneak into the set, the ground floor of the inn, without anyone seeing me, and to set up my two attaché cases, I had to be there two hours earlier than anyone else. Since I couldn't sew myself into the saris, I wore my plain black evening gown. With no sari to cover my practically bare everything on top and my holster in back, I had to put on my long-sleeve black jacket so that I looked like my grandmother from the olden days. Of course, very few grandmothers from the olden days carried guns in their belt holsters, but I was also a private eye from today, and a gun was part of the uniform. By keeping my head down, I was just a black shadow against the wall of the inn.

I had spent all day getting my lights ready. Alexander had just told me to get lights. Nothing to it, right? Later, I would tell him what that entailed. And what it cost. It was my brilliant scheme to get flashes, camera flashes. They give more light per cubic inch of volume than anything else you can get retail, and four dozen fit into an attaché case easily. The only trouble is, the flashes are of very short duration, and it takes several seconds for a flash to recycle. So the camera store fastened them together in four sets of twelve each, the most powerful small flashes they had, and wired them to a—I memorized it—to a pair of battery-operated, twenty-four-pole, rotary, sequential switches, so that, when I pressed the button on the hand-held switch, there'd be four flashes a second. Like a stroboscope. Not exactly what Alexander had in mind, but bright enough to light up the Statue of Liberty at ten paces, the salesman assured me, and to keep flashing for a good fifteen minutes, minimum. Batteries were extra. Since Gilda was only about fifteen feet away from me, and that's where I had to aim the lights, I wasn't worried. The salesman even put little pieces of black tape over the tiny "ready" lights on the flashes, so they wouldn't give away my position. No extra charge.

Alexander loved the setup. He put me against a post on the outside wall of the inn, the one just to the left of the one that had the candle and light that were shining on Gilda, Pearl. There were two sets of flash assemblies on each side of me; only about a foot long each and six inches high, sitting on the floor and tilted up. I was sure no one in the audience could see them through the scrim. I had the foresight to bring a small canvas folding stool; two hours of sitting on the floor would have paralyzed me. I did it all in the dark—nothing was on when I got there—so I had to use a penlight. For two hours— every little noise—it got so I was reaching for my gun every ten minutes.

Just before eight—my watch was in my bag so the glow wouldn't give me away—Alexander, using a penlight and carefully keeping the light shining away from me, took Carlo Cacciare upstairs. Alexander then brought in Brezhnikov and set him near the fireplace, facing the entrance of the inn. Then he came in with Pearl, dressed as Gilda, helped her into the sack, and leaned her against the center post, her head down, her long golden hair—her own, not a wig—hanging down over her face. Last, he brought in Salome Auber, set her halfway up the stairs opposite Gilda, and told her to wait there until her musical cue, then to continue upstairs. He lit the candle in her left hand and faced her toward my left, ready to go upstairs.

Alexander pulled over a chair from the table in the middle of the inn and stood on it to light the candle on the outside wall shelf opposite Gilda, keeping his back to me to shield me from what little light might come my way. Without using his penlight, he put the chair back and left the set. A few seconds later, the candlelight increased tenfold. Alexander must have had the console operator turn up the little light next to the wall candle to the same brightness as during the performance. I could see Pearl clearly.

The outside lighting, the moonlight, came on. The stage was set exactly as it had been the night Thea Malabar had been murdered. The candle flickered, striking dim sparks from Pearl's golden hair. It was so scary, I switched the light button to my left hand and took my gun out of the holster. I held the little gun in my lap, under my bag, ready. For what, I didn't know, but ready.

The audiotape started, the storm music. At the height of the storm I heard Gilda knock at the door, three times. At the third knock, I heard Maddalena let her in. The door squeaked, the tape was so clear, and I could hear, even, the rustle of the canvas thrown over Gilda's head. Sparafucile stabbed Gilda, and her scream was so real I felt shivers up my back and my legs chilled. The storm began to die down and Salome went upstairs.

My neck was really stiff, and I turned my head a little, slowly, so as not to be noticed. As I did, I saw . . . something. Out of the corner of my eye I saw a something. Turning back, I tried to see it more clearly, but it wasn't there. Just blackness. Then the blackness moved; I knew it moved. Not a shadow. The blackness moved, I *knew* it. It was directly opposite me and it moved, definitely. I saw it. Not a shadow, a blackness. Moving. Moving toward Gilda. Pearl. My Pearl. The blackness was moving very slowly, but it was moving. Now that I knew where it was, I could see, sense, see it moving. To Pearl. To *kill* Pearl. The shadow, the *blackness,* was very close to Pearl. Why didn't Alexander yell "Lights!"? What was he waiting for? Didn't he know the blackness was going to—? Where *was* Alexander? Outside, Rigoletto was singing "The Moment of My Revenge Has Come at Last."

The shadow, the blackness, was almost on Pearl. Then I saw the glint, the *knife,* it was a *knife,* the blackness was going to *kill* Pearl. I couldn't wait; I pressed the light button.

The lights exploded, flash-flash-flash—so *bright*—flash-

211

flash—*too* bright—flash, like lightning. The black bulk near Pearl turned to me, the knife throwing back the brilliant flashes, like slow motion, like stroboscopic motion. Pearl was screaming, Rigoletto was singing, enjoying his revenge, while Pearl was screaming and the knife was flashing, flashing . . . Then, behind the black bulk I saw another black bulk, even bigger, with a *knife*, another *knife*, a flashing *knife*, opposite me. The second black bulk turned to me and *screamed*, knife lifted, and began to come at *me*. Not at Pearl, at *me*. With his knife raised at *me*. I lifted the gun and pulled the trigger. Nothing happened. Again, again, I pulled the trigger—the lights flashed—zip-zip-zip—and the drummer was banging rim shots—tap-tap-tap—and the lights were flashing—zip-zip—and the black bulk was almost on top of me and the knife—and I kept squeezing the trigger but the gun wouldn't fire—and the lights were stabbing—zip-zip—and the drummer—tap-tap—why wouldn't it fire?—tap-tap—and the black bulk lunged at me in slow motion and the knife stretched out and—zip-zip—fell down with the knife—fell down with the knife cutting down right through my good black evening gown—my only black evening gown—cutting down right between my knees—cutting down, sticking in the floor—the wooden floor—right between my knees—cutting down and the lights went out.

37

Alexander was holding me and crying, getting tear stains all over my only long-sleeved black jacket. "I didn't think," he sobbed. "He wasn't supposed to . . . It was just to show . . ." Somebody had turned all the lights on, inside and outside of the inn. Burton and Pearl came over too and held me. Pearl was crying, spoiling her beautiful makeup. Burton pushed us all away from the body, the knife still sticking upright in the floor, the hand, the big hand, the dead hand half-curled on the floor next to the knife.

"Why are his feet green?" I asked. "His shoes? On the bottom?"

"Later," Burton said. "Let's get outside." He led me through the front door of the inn, down the two steps, to the edge of the river, the black river, as far from the inn as we could get.

"Sit down," Burton said. "A chair. Get a chair," he told Sparafucile. Brezhnikov hesitated, then ran back into the inn.

"What was that on his head?" I asked. Carlo Cacciare and Salome Auber came over, saying something. I don't understand Italian. Or fast French.

Hugo Kreuz brought me a glass. "Drink it," he ordered.

"Fast." It was hot and it burned. I choked, coughed. He filled the glass again. *"Noch ein mal,"* he said. I didn't want to, but he held it to my mouth and I had to. This time I didn't choke. Alexander held me as I sat down.

"Too big to be Zacharias," I said.

"It's all right, darling," Alexander said. "It's all right. He was going to kill *me.*"

The auditorium lights were up. Everybody was standing. They were all looking at me. I felt so ashamed. Warshafsky was telling the audience to go home. Nobody made a move. They were all watching me. I didn't want them to see me. I pulled Alexander in front of me.

"Valczyk?" I knew. "Jan Valczyk."

"He tried to kill you, darling," Alexander said. "When the lights flashed, he went crazy. He tried to kill you. There was no point." Alexander sounded bewildered; why would anyone do something so illogical? "Once I demonstrated . . . There was no *point.*"

"I killed him, didn't I? The gun worked, didn't it? The drummer—? Take me home." I didn't feel good. "I didn't want to kill him. I just wanted . . . Take me home, Alexander. Please."

38

Alexander made me take a Valium, in spite of my having drunk Kreuz's two brandies, and Pearl had given me a hot bath and a flannel nightgown and a warm bathrobe and a big towel around my head. She had put a big glass of hot tea with honey and lemon on the kitchen table in front of me. Alexander she gave strong cocoa, very brown, and Burt and Minos Zacharias had black coffee. I didn't feel too glamorous, but I was beginning to feel, so it was okay.

"He attached the green insoles," Alexander said—"you can get them in any drugstore—to the soles of his shoes with makeup gum. So his footsteps would be silent."

"Why didn't the police find them?" Burton asked. "I know they searched everybody."

"He put them back into his shoes after he killed Thea Malabar."

"But they can't fit," Burton said. "The gum is on the wrong side of the inner soles."

"They're on the right side if you flip them over," Alexander said. "He put the sole from his left shoe into his right shoe, and vice versa. Try it, you'll see. The gum on the bottom held them in place inside his shoes. Even if he was strip searched, no one would see anything wrong. Whatever gum was stuck to the bottom of his shoes, he rubbed off into dust with his hands."

"And the black cloth on his head?" Pearl asked. "And on yours?"

"Black scrim. Tons of it in the prop room. The whole front of the inn was black scrim. You could see out of it but nobody could see in. He picked up a scrap and sewed it into a sort of sack and dickey, and kept it in his pocket. It folds very small. When he was ready, he went around the corner of the back of the set and slipped it over his head and shirt front. Staying close to the black-painted flats, he slipped into the light trap leading into the inn. No one was going to use that entrance, for any reason at all, after Sparafucile entered. When he was done with the scrim sack, he slipped out the thread holding it together, and it was just another scrap of scrim again."

"And you did the same?" Pearl asked.

"I can't sew. I stapled mine together."

"What about his hands?" Minos Zacharias asked. "No gloves were found."

"He didn't need gloves. He entered the inn as soon as Maddalena started upstairs. His left hand was in his pocket and it was on the side away from the audience anyway. His right hand was holding the knife under his jacket. He reached Thea Malabar just as she finished telling Salome she was going to have her killed. He grabbed Thea's face with his left hand, from around the pole, covering her nose and mouth so she couldn't make a sound, or even breathe, and pushed the knife in with his right. Against her blond hair, his hand was almost invisible; a black-gloved hand would have shown up easily."

"Then the glint you saw on the videotapes—?" Pearl asked.

"The knife, just as I thought. He held her that way for about ten seconds, then let her head down slowly, naturally, still holding her nose and mouth, and pushed the knife in with his fist."

"That wiped off all the fingerprints," Burton added.

"Yes, and if there was any blood, whatever little there may have been, he could rub or wash it off. Don't forget, he had at least ten minutes to dump the scrim in the prop room, go to the bathroom, do whatever he wanted."

"I still can't believe no one saw him."

"A man wearing white tie and tails is highly visible. But if you cover the white areas with black, and put him against a dark background in poor light, and he moves slowly, making sure he never passes between a viewer and a source of light, he is, for all practical purposes, invisible. In that scene, there was no light coming from the back wall of the inn, except for the fireplace, which was quite far away, to silhouette a figure. The only light shining inside the inn was the leakage of dim moonlight from the exterior, and the light from the candle and adjoining dim bulb opposite Malabar. Which was narrowly focused on Malabar. Valczyk didn't reflect any light, he was a shadow against darkness; an invisible man."

"Do you mean that he set up the whole opera this way," Minos Zacharias asked, "just to kill Thea Malabar?"

"Certainly not," Alexander said. "This production of *Rigoletto* was three years in the planning. Valczyk merely took advantage of the circumstances. I don't think he decided to kill Thea until a couple of weeks ago."

"I just remembered," Pearl said, "we were so upset before . . . Thank you for taking us home in your limousine, Mr. Zacharias. Especially after we all thought . . . I mean—"

"That's quite all right," he said, graciously. "You weren't the only one who thought . . . How did you figure it out, Gold?"

"I remembered, in my talk with Salome Auber, that I mentioned ultraviolet light, which is often called black light, because ultraviolet light is beyond the spectrum of human vision. We cannot see it at all. That reminded me of The Black Light Theater of Prague, an unusual and remarkable troupe of actors and puppeteers who have given performances all over the world. Against a black background they have people completely dressed in black who are, therefore, completely invisible. These people move props, puppets, and even actors around; they cover the props and actors, and uncover them, with black cloths. They handle the puppets, do whatever is required. It looks as though the props and puppets are moving by themselves, or floating magically. There are also visible actors and props, made visible by being painted or made up with fluorescent paint, paint that glows under ultraviolet light. You can't imagine what can be done with this: Actors floating in midair, objects flying around the stage, people appearing and disappearing . . . their special effects have to be seen to be believed."

That must have been what Alexander called the artist's representative about this morning. God, was it only this morning?

"And Jan Valczyk saw this company?" Minos asked.

"I'm sure he did, it was organized in '62, and may even have been instrumental, he was a small boy then, in his later interest in puppetry. But whether he saw them in Prague, or in Edinburgh, or wherever, I'm sure he knew about them. He was always interested in puppets; did his dissertation on Oriental puppetry, and traveled extensively in the Far East, studying Eastern puppet styles. This led me naturally to Bunraku, the classical Japanese puppet theater. Bunraku uses large puppets, half-to three-quarters life size. These puppets are moved on stage by puppeteers who are usually—guess what?—dressed entirely in black. They operate in full view of the audience and, I understand, become psychologically invisible in a few minutes. If they were put against a black background, even in average light, they'd be truly invisible. So it was obvious that the murderer was Jan Valczyk. The technique of the murder was equally obvious."

"But why did he try to kill you?" Pearl asked. "In spite of

what you figured out, there was no way to prove anything. You said so yourself. All he had to do was nothing, and he couldn't have been arrested."

"It wasn't that easy," Alexander said. "I was going to demonstrate how Thea Malabar was murdered. As soon as I had the knife near Gilda's throat, Pearl's, I would have signaled Norma to put on the lights. Then I would have taken off my scrim sack. This demonstration would have shown the police how it was done."

"But there was no proof," Burton objected. "None at all."

"With what the police knew of everyone's background and movements, it would have been easy to check that at the moment of the murder—the glint of the knife on the videotape, remember?—that only Valczyk was unaccounted for. They would have arrested him and sweated him, interrogated him for a week. He might have broken."

"No way," Burton said. "He wouldn't have said a word and the police would have had to release him. He'd never have been indicted."

"Maybe, but the police would have closed the case, we'd have gotten paid, and everyone would have known that Valczyk had killed Malabar."

"You mean, *I* would have known," Minos Zacharias said. "You were depending on me to have . . . to have him taken care of."

"Wouldn't you have had to?" Alexander asked.

"I don't wish to discuss this," Zacharias said.

"I still don't see"—Burton looked puzzled—"how killing you would solve any of Valczyk's problems. With you lying there in that black scrim sack, he's in the same position as before. Worse."

"Of course," Alexander said. "But Valczyk didn't intend to kill me onstage; he intended to kill me in the light trap."

"Wouldn't that be dangerous to him too?" Burton asked. "Everybody but Valczyk and Kreuz would be eliminated as suspects."

"Cacciare would be; he was upstairs. But anyone who was backstage for a minute or two could have done it: Rigoletto and Sparafucile, for example. Even Maddalena, provided Sparafucile covered for her. So we'd still have D'Aquilla, Brezhnikov, and Salome Auber."

"The timing," Pearl said. "Wouldn't the medical examiner be able to tell you were stabbed"—she shivered at this—"at the time all the singers were onstage?"

"The medical examiner," Burton explained, "can't pinpoint time of death within minutes, so that wouldn't clear anyone. But I still don't see why killing Alex would save Valczyk."

"Valczyk didn't believe that I really knew how it was done," Alexander said, "and we did broadcast that I didn't know who did it. But he had to be prepared. He would keep his eye on the light trap, and if he saw me go in—if you're really looking for it, you can see the blackness moving—he would enter right behind me, stab me, take off my black scrim sack, and presto, another insoluble mystery."

"And you set yourself up for this?" Pearl was horrified.

"Certainly not." Alexander was indignant. "Once in the light trap, I walked backwards, waving my knife in front of me. Valczyk couldn't have come near me without getting cut in half."

"Then why didn't he?" Pearl asked. "Try to kill you in the light trap, I mean."

"When he killed Thea Malabar, he was not in a hurry. As long as he reached her before Sparafucile dragged the sack out, there was no problem. So when Kreuz saw Valczyk backstage, they exchanged a few words. Then Valczyk went around the corner, became invisible, and completed the job. But I ordered that everyone do the same thing tonight that they did on the night of the murder, and Kreuz, with typical German thoroughness, insisted on talking to Valczyk for a minute, using exactly the same words, I'll bet. Ask him. Valczyk couldn't refuse—what would he be in a hurry for that he could explain to Kreuz?—so by the time he got to the light trap, I was already halfway to Gilda."

"Then what was the point in killing you near Gilda?" Pearl asked. "Near me?"

"After he stabbed me, he could whip off my scrim sack and disappear again. I would suddenly have appeared out of nowhere, a knife in my back, and the mystery of who killed Thea Malabar would still be unsolved, with an additional mystery added. But he didn't know about Norma and the lights. The shock was too much for him, given the tension he was under and the requirement to suddenly change his plans. He's well known for making very detailed plans, and blowing his top if they're frustrated in any way."

"Still," Pearl said, "you were setting yourself up as bait. That's crazy."

"I never expected him to try to kill me. I thought, when he realized I knew how it was done, he would run away. And"—he took my hand—"I could never have figured he would try to hurt Norma, or that if *anyone* would, I could not stop him."

"Can you imagine," Burton said, clearly trying to get off the subject of Valczyk's attack on me, "what the papers would have done if Valczyk had succeeded?" Latching onto Alexander's murder was no great improvement. "And the TV? As it is, half the news today is about the murder of Thea Malabar, about *Rigoletto,* interviews with opera critics, Pantheon executives, no end. A second mysterious murder on stage would have meant six-inch headlines. Around the world."

"That may have had something to do with it too," Pearl said. "Why Valczyk used his own production as a way to kill Thea

Malabar. You couldn't buy that much publicity for a million dollars. Ten million. Anybody in the theater would kill for that alone."

"I'm sure," Alexander said, "unconsciously, it had some influence on Valczyk; he had to be aware of the sensation it would cause. But as a motive to kill someone, to risk your own life? Only a psychopath would do that, and Valczyk was no psychopath."

"The motive," Minos Zacharias said. "*Why* did he kill her? The reason has become very important to me."

"Do you really want to know?" Alexander asked gently.

"I must know," Minos said. "Everything depends on it."

Alexander took a deep breath. "The motive puzzled me too, even after I knew the who and the how. For this I applied pure logic, reasoning backwards. There is no way I can prove what I say, but there is no other explanation that fits."

"You are saying"—Minos grew excited—"that Thea Malabar did not kill Helen?"

"It doesn't figure," Alexander said. "Helen never stood in your way with regard to Thea. Had you wanted a divorce, even, she would have given it to you. It would have lost you half, or more, of your business, but you could have had a divorce for the asking, and I think you knew that."

"I didn't want a divorce," Zacharias said. "Thea understood that, I believe."

"Helen was big and strong; Thea small and weak. Is it likely that Thea could have pushed Helen overboard? Possible, yes," Alexander said, "but not very probable. Then too, your wife, Minos, was a good swimmer. Strong. Even if Thea Malabar could have pushed her overboard, why was she not found floating when they found her scarf?"

"Malabar could have hit her on the head with a club," Pearl said, "or something like a club. A hammer, maybe. That's how

Malabar could have done it and that's why Helen wasn't found."

"Even if she could get a hammer," Alexander replied, "it's not likely she could approach Helen carrying a weapon. Even if she could, would she be able to hit Helen? Helen was an athlete; her reactions had to be twice as fast as Thea Malabar's."

"Maybe Thea found Helen leaning over the rail," Pearl suggested.

"Can you see Thea Malabar wandering around the deck with a hammer hidden in the bodice of her gown, hoping to find Helen Zacharias leaning over the rail?" Alexander shook his head. "Further, Thea understood that she would be the most likely suspect under the conditions that existed that night. Not that she feared the police, but she knew what Demetrios Taramakis could do."

"I wondered, at first, why he did not kill her," Zacharias said; "then I realized he was waiting for proof that I put her up to it, so he could kill us both."

"You knew it was he who was forcing you back to Greece?"

"I knew. There were too many coincidences. He *wanted* me to know. I put it off as long as I could, but there comes a time . . . That's why I stood for your insults, Gold. Another time . . . I think there will be respect on both sides, Alexander."

"I'm sure of it, Minos."

"Tell me, then, why did Valczyk kill my wife?"

"My agreement with you, Zacharias, was limited to the murder of Thea Malabar. That was the way you wanted it."

"You want more money, Gold?"

"No. I will tell you, if you really want. But don't ask; I urge you not to ask."

"I insist. I must know."

Alexander hesitated, then said, simply, "Helen was pregnant. She and Valczyk had been having an affair. Since Glyndebourne,

I believe. Her love for children was well known and, accidentally, she would get her wish. She *wanted* to have a baby; that baby, and at her age, it was the last chance she would get. Since you are sterile, publicly, she could not pass it off as yours, even if you agreed. So she decided to divorce you and marry Valczyk."

"You are sure of this?" Zacharias' face was gray.

"That she was pregnant, yes. I spoke to Taramakis early today. He still had Helen's personal maid in his employ. In reserve, so to speak, for the time when he would check your statements with her. He asked for the name and address; there was no way the maid could refuse him. He spoke to the doctor Helen used in Edinburgh. The doctor told him, not for money or out of fear, but out of compassion for the dead woman's father."

"And Valczyk was the father?"

"I have no proof of this, but given the circumstances, it seems evident."

"If she had only told me. We could have arranged . . . something. That is the one thing I would have given her a divorce for, had she come to me *before* she got pregnant. It would have cost me heavily, in many ways, but I would not have stood in her way."

"I'm sure she knew that, Minos, as I'm sure she never would have asked you, knowing what it would have meant to you psychologically. But when it happened . . . *She* set up the yacht trip, with the opera as an excuse, and arranged your business affairs so you had to go to Crete, so she could persuade Valczyk to go along with her plans. Although he genuinely liked her, he did not want to marry, and was particularly afraid to marry her, was very frightened that you would kill him for betraying you with Helen."

"I would not have," Zacharias said, "I think. And I would never deny Helen anything she really wanted."

"But Valczyk didn't know that. He told Helen he would not marry her. She said she would have the baby anyway. She had wanted a baby desperately, her own baby; it was the only thing missing from her life. Not that she had gotten pregnant deliberately—she would never do that to you—but now that it was here, she would go ahead. Valczyk knew what that meant: That sooner or later you would find out he was the father, that he had cuckolded you, and that you would have to kill him. The pressure was too great. He panicked, as he did tonight. He struck Helen, hard, knocking her overboard, unconscious. Otherwise, could not a strong swimmer, as she was, stay afloat for a half-hour, an hour, easily, in the warm waters of the summer Mediterranean?"

"And Thea saw this?"

"It's obvious. She decided to keep her mouth shut, and use the knowledge. She backed up Valczyk's story and didn't say a word until they were back on dry land; she didn't want to go overboard too."

"But she blackmailed him," Zacharias said, "didn't she?"

"Only for money, I'm sure, and relatively small amounts at that. Not that she needed the money, although she *was* greedy, but more to remind Valczyk who had the whip hand. She sensed, I think, that if she attacked his art, his true love, that he would have rebelled."

"Then why did he kill her, Gold?"

"Just before she was killed, Thea threatened Salome Auber. She didn't say, 'I'll kill you' or 'I'll get you for that.' Thea said, 'I'm going to have you killed.' *Have you killed.* By someone else. Thea had a weapon, a murderer she controlled, or thought she controlled. Someone she could make kill for her."

"He could have refused."

"Then Thea would have told Demetrios Taramakis who killed his only child. Valczyk would have been dead in a week. The hard way."

"Had Valczyk killed for Thea before?"

"No."

"So Thea had ordered Valczyk to kill someone?"

"Yes."

"Recently?"

"Yes."

"And Valczyk didn't want to do it?"

"That's right."

"He refused her?"

"No. He couldn't do that; it would mean his death. But he was able to foresee her demands escalating; with Thea Malabar, there were no limits. Next would be Ettore D'Aquilla, then Salome Auber, Carlo Cacciare, Hugo Kreuz, who knows? Valczyk knew he had no choice. The only way out was to kill Thea Malabar. He figured out how to do it, and he did."

"Who did she want him to kill, Gold?" Alexander did not answer. He just looked at Zacharias. "Me? She wanted him to kill *me?* That's crazy. Why?"

"You were going to marry Patricia Horgan instead of Thea Malabar."

"But she knew why. She knew that—"

"All she knew was that, with your wife out of the way, you weren't preparing to marry her."

Minos Zacharias sat for a while, deep in thought. He stood up, raising himself heavily, looking his age for the first time since I met him. "You have done a good job, Gold," he said. "It was not *what* I wanted, not *how* I wanted, but a good job nevertheless. You have, probably, saved my life, though I would have preferred you did it in a different way. You have also brought me great unhappiness."

"You insisted on knowing," Alexander said.

"You could have refused to tell me, Gold."

"Someone else would have told you; you would have searched for the truth. Better from me."

"Not better, Gold; just not as bad. I must go." He glanced at his watch. "I must make some calls early tomorrow morning."

"Burton Hanslik will call Demetrios Taramakis shortly," Alexander said. "Taramakis is waiting for the call. Do you want to talk to him from here? I will give you privacy."

"I might have known, Gold." Minos Zacharias shook his huge bull's head slowly. "No. No, tell him I will call him tomorrow, after he has slept. I will visit him in Athens to pay my respects, as is fitting, before I go to Crete. And we will mourn together. Good-bye."

"Like a classic Greek tragedy," Pearl said. "It was foreordained. Everything. Once it was started, there was no way to stop it." She and Burton started downstairs to the office to call Athens. "I'll call Julia Baron too," Pearl said at the door. "She deserves it."

"I'll have to get another black evening gown," I told Alexander.

He put his arm around me. "I'll go with you."

"I didn't mean to kill him," I said. "I really didn't."

"I know," my husband said. "I know."

(